SOUL TO KEEP

VAMPIRE SORORITY SISTERS
BOOK 3

What Reviewers Say About Rebekah Weatherspoon's Work

Better Off Red

"Rebekah Weatherspoon has crafted a feisty little debut that forever changes the image of sororities in lesbian literature."
—*The Rainbow Reader*

The Fling

"I loved this book from start to finish and I'm so glad I have more of Ms. Weatherspoon's books to read."—*Rainbow Book Reviews*

At Her Feet

"Indeed, the more I read *At Her Feet* I came to realize that it is the best and most original book that I have read in any genre for a very long time."—Jim Lyons, *The Seattle Post-Intelligencer*

Visit us at www.boldstrokesbooks.com

By the Author

Vampire Sorority Sisters Series

Better Off Red

Blacker Than Blue

Soul to Keep

The Fling

At Her Feet

Treasure

SOUL TO KEEP

VAMPIRE SORORITY SISTERS
BOOK 3

by

Rebekah Weatherspoon

2016

This Trade Paperback Original Is Published By
Bold Strokes Books, Inc.
P.O. Box 249
Valley Falls, NY 12185

First Edition: March 2016

Credits
Editor: Cindy Cresap
Production Design: Susan Ramundo
Cover Design By Sheri (graphicartist2020@hotmail.com)

Acknowledgments

Thank you to the team at Bold Strokes Books. Cindy, Sandy, and Rad, thank you for putting up with me and my weak comprehension of the word deadline.

Dedication

This one is for you, the readers, who have been waiting for this next installment. Thank you for being patient with me while I got to know Jill and Tokyo.

Alpha Beta Omega Sorority
Founded 1863
Community Through Sisterhood and Service
Pro Maius Bonum

CHAPTER ONE

Jill, October, Fall Semester

> *Dr. Miller,*
> *Thank you for your prompt response, but I do not believe "this is something we should revisit some other time." When you offered to let your classes come up with presentations covering topics of health and public safety in place of a final, I did not for one moment think that you meant this to be a fruitless exercise to keep you from grading papers or exams. You are asking that we put in a tremendous amount of effort in designing these presentations, and I—*

"What are you typing?" Camila asked.

"An email."

"To who? You're about to type the keys right off that thing."

I liked Camila, but I kind of wanted her to mind her own business. "No, I won't. I just have to get a point across."

Camila came over to the chaise I was sitting on and peered over my shoulder. For a vampire who could read anyone's thoughts, it seemed unnecessary and rude. "Here." I stopped just long enough to turn the screen in her direction. She only needed a second to glance at the response I was sending to my Human Sexuality professor.

Camila stood there as I kept typing.

—am simply asking for assistance in creating a presentation that can actually be implemented at the university as a program with ongoing potential to educate thousands of students for years to come.

I do not need to reiterate how the majority of students attending Maryland University come from schools, both public and private, who had nothing of a sex ed program. I also do not think I need to tell you that while the number of HIV infections in some populations are on the decline, rates of STIs such as chlamydia are in fact on the rise. The number of cases of HPV on this very campus has tripled in the last ten years. It took me over four man hours, fifteen phone calls, and five in-person visits to the university health center to acquire this information, so you can see when a program such as the one that I've outlined for you in my previous—

"You sure you want to send that?" Camila asked. I should have finished this in my room, but when your vampire calls, you come. Camila was not my vampire. If she were, I wouldn't have been short with her for being so nosy. If she were, she would be feeding from me at that moment instead of asking about private business between my shortsighted professor and me.

"Of course I want to send it. I wouldn't waste my time typing it up if I was going to keep it all to myself and my trash bin."

"Red can't keep you from getting booted from a class, ya know."

"Babe, leave her alone. And, yes, I can." I looked up as Ginger came into the room. My heart skipped a beat. It always did when I saw her. My blood actually rushed in my veins, no exaggeration there. When my future sorority sisters tried to explain the power of their connections with their vampires, I didn't fully believe it. I didn't believe my body or my heart would react so strongly, but once our covenant was sealed with blood and a kiss, I couldn't imagine having any other reaction to Ginger. Just the sight of my blood-bound supernatural being made my chest seize on itself from pure excitement, and for a split second I couldn't breathe. That reaction, the intense clarity of it, defined what it meant to be claimed as a feeder. But the feeling faded the moment I saw what Ginger was wearing.

"You're not even dressed! At least Camila's dressed." They stood there, looking at me, Camila draped in a long black robe, and Ginger, completely naked. I stared back at them.

"Jill, sweetie. We're leaving as soon as I feed."

"Okay, I just need to finish this e-mail. It's more than a grade. This could change the whole new student orientation program and boost the overall wellness of the entire university."

"Jill. We have to go. Just pause for two seconds with the typing and then you can turn this whole school around. You can change the world."

"Where are you going again?" I asked.

"Samantha is becoming one of us tonight. It's her rebirth," Ginger said.

"Why now? We just finished initiation. The new girls are barely acclimated to how we do things. Wouldn't you rather stay here with them?" I asked.

"You mean wouldn't I rather stay here with you."

"No. Bonding with you was important for me. I'm sure the new girls want that too."

From what I understood, humans didn't become vampires very often. Clearly, it was a special occasion, but this semester's fall pledge class had just joined Alpha Beta Omega Sorority. It seemed like a horrible time to bring a fresh vampire into their fold. I glanced up at Camila as the thought crossed my mind. She wasn't very subtle with the way she glared in my direction, but I think she agreed with me.

"We'll bond plenty." Ginger picked me up and swung me effortlessly into her lap, then she took my laptop out of my hands. "Sam is going through the biggest change of her life, and I need to be in top shape for the occasion so give me that neck."

"I don't know why you'd want to change her. She's not very nice." I hadn't seen Samantha in two years, but she'd been horrible to me my freshman year. That wasn't something I would ever forget.

"She has a point," Camila said.

"Both of you, please. Shut up. Jill. Vein. Now."

I tilted my head to the side with a bit of a groan, but still offered her my neck.

Our feedings seemed to always start out the same way. Ginger interrupting me and me being frustrated with being interrupted. School and the sorority kept me busy, but I'd made a pledge and a promise, and Ginger needed sustenance so she wouldn't go crazy from blood lust and kill us all. I understood. I really did, and I was grateful to serve her, but I hadn't applied to schools in the States, enrolled in Maryland University, and left my dad and papa behind in Montreal to join a sorority whose only function was to feed a select group of vampires. That just sort of happened.

It *was* an ingenious cover. Stash your vampires at select schools all over the world so you can discreetly funnel more humans into your food chain. Plus the sorority would look great on my med school applications, but I had *a lot* of studying to do, and I had to get this situation with Dr. Miller taken care of before she wasted more of my time.

I tried to think of how to drive my point home with my professor, and then Ginger's fangs pierced my throat. I came instantly, forgetting all about Dr. Miller and our frustrating back-and-forth.

Ginger's fangs were huge—thick, sharp points that made clean incisions into the carotid artery. I asked her about it once, how it worked and how she managed not to kill one of us with every feeding. It would have been so easy. Once she was in, I was useless in her hands, a pile of writhing mush for the taking. She could have easily ended my life or the lives of any of her humans, because we never wanted her to stop. Though I supposed that would defeat the purpose of having dedicated feeders.

The bond and the orgasms brought me back, three times a week, giving her what she needed to take. Something in their saliva, or something in the magic that made them what they were, triggered that initial climax. And that climax continued, not in waves though. It was more like a loop. While she fed, I just kept coming and coming and coming. I was bound to her by that magic, but the chemicals that flooded my body with each drop of blood I gave up were like drugs that kept me coming back.

Sometimes she touched me over my clothes, but tonight I just let her hold me until she was done. When her lips released my throat for a split second, I tried to remember what I had to do next. Everything was a little foggy until I looked up and saw Camila standing in their bedroom doorway. They had somewhere to be, and I had an e-mail to finish. And an Arabic exam to study for and a lab report to finish.

I held on to Ginger, let her hold on to me, even after the final wave of pleasure rushed over my body. I felt her tongue seal the punctures in my neck and then she kissed me. Same as always, a few soft, gentle kisses on my lips and my cheeks as she thanked me. When I pulled away, her green eyes had a slight glow to them and her freckled face was flushed. She glanced from me to Camila, as she stroked my back.

"I should have fed you after," I said. She didn't look like she was in any condition to go anywhere. And I knew when she was giving her wife the "Do Me Now" eye. I didn't have sex with Ginger the way some of the other girls did when it came to their vampires, but I did like cuddling with her after she fed. Camila would join us a lot of the time, and they would tease me about making a Jill sandwich. Until I remembered I had work to do and ditched them so I could study and they could hump each other.

Ginger kissed my forehead then set me on my feet. I was still a little wobbly. "If you're up when we get back—"

"No, don't bother," I said, waving her off. "I have my eight a.m."

"I'll come say good night when I come back anyway. Or you can stay down here."

I shrugged in agreement and flopped back down on the couch. I really just needed to catch my breath and get my mind together before I got back to my e-mail. My body was still coming a little. Ginger and Camila finished getting ready, buzzing about the room, almost forgetting I was there. Ginger was worried about Samantha, she told Camila.

I stretched, squeezing my eyes shut, thinking of how I could help make things easier for Sam's rebirth, even though I knew I couldn't. When I opened my eyes, our sister-queen Faeth appeared. Then Omi, Natasha, and Kina followed behind her. They were all naked. Well, basically naked. They wore these loincloth type things made of black diamonds, and ornate black diamond necklaces. They'd worn similar jewelry for our initiations, but instead of black diamonds, their bodies were draped in rubies, like the teardrop ruby I wore around my neck, the symbol of my commitment to Ginger and the rest of the girls. The second they noticed me on the couch, they all greeted me with warm smiles and hellos.

Camila came out of the bedroom, securing her own necklace. "All good?"

"All the girls are in the house, and Pax and Malcolm will be keeping an eye on things while we're gone," Omi said.

"Where's Tokyo?" Ginger called from the bedroom.

"Uh..."

"What the fuck?" Ginger said, storming into the living room. She handed her own adornments to Camila and turned around so Camila could connect the shiny chain of diamonds around her hips. "She knew we had to leave exactly at ten." The clock on their cable box said nine fifty-five.

"Faeth," Ginger said.

"Yeah."

"Please go get her."

"Oh, do I have to? I hate going down there. Moreland's gonna try to get me to stay."

"Faeth," Camila added. Ginger was in charge, but everyone, all the vampires, me, and the girls included, knew how things worked. Camila always backed Ginger up.

"Fine." Faeth vanished, the sound of her sighing trailed behind her.

Ginger came back over to the couch and kissed me one more time. "We have to go. Don't stay up too late."

"I won't."

"Love you," she said with a wink.

Then they all vanished, off to their vampire business.

I looked around the sprawling living room, thinking about the even larger apartment attached to it, and the six other apartments, and the winding hallways and other rooms and corners that were home to our sister-queens. Thousands of square feet hidden underneath the school's Greek Row. I thought about just how empty those rooms were at the moment, and suddenly, I didn't see the point of staying on the bottom floor all by myself. I grabbed my stuff and headed back up toward my room.

And then I remembered it was Monday night, aka Alpha Beta Omega Sorority's designated porn night. It started as a joke to freak out incoming freshmen, but now it was a weekly event where the girls would gather around the Apple TV to find the grossest, weirdest, most ridiculous porn to pick apart for an hour or so before they remembered it was Monday and we had class the next day. Things upstairs would be loud and out of control for a while longer. And then at some point things would turn serious, and the girls would pair off or into their feeder clusters and act like sleeping with each other was something they would do even if they weren't magically blood bound, inhibitions stripped.

I flopped back down in the closest armchair so I could finish my e-mail in peace.

CHAPTER TWO

Tokyo

"Why'd you stop?" I growled, pissed as hell. "I was almost there."

"Well, quite suddenly, we are not alone, my dear." Moreland's Southern drawl came next to my ear, right before she nipped my shoulder with her fangs. We'd been at it for a few hours, my vampire friend and I, pushing the pretend boundaries of our sexual limits. If there wasn't somewhere I was *required* to be by vampire law, we'd have gone at it until sunrise. But responsibilities and all that bullshit.

I loved my girls. All of my feeders, but at least three times a week, there was something—a meeting, a curfew check, another meeting, a rebirth ceremony—something that required me to put my life on hold so I could show up and be counted. I got it, okay? Being immortal was pretty fucking sweet. The perks were endless. The sex was amazing, and when we weren't on a conference call about what the girls needed or some pointless event, or mundane happening, that amazing sex was practically nonstop.

And yes, I'd volunteered to assist our Master by serving under his Alpha sister-queen in her nest, but when I agreed to move in to take on the members of ABO as feeders, I had no idea just how much those responsibilities would cramp the shit out of my style. Half the time, I felt like I had six demanding employees and six micromanaging supervisors. I couldn't catch a fucking break.

I vanished out of my restraints and over to my jeans that were draped on Moreland's couch. I didn't need to look up to see that we weren't alone. I could scent my sister-in-blood-and-misery from a few miles away.

"Tell your highnesses I'll be right there," I said.

"I can't leave without you." I glanced up at the awkward tightness in Faeth's voice. She was an easy six feet two in her natural form, but in the world of immortals she was still a baby vampire. Moreland and I were old.

"Care for a beverage while you wait? I can have one of my boys fetch it for you," Moreland offered. She wasn't wearing much. Just a bra and the strap-on dildo she'd been teasing me with.

"I'm fine. T, let's go."

"Jesus. Coming." I kissed Moreland on both cheeks—she knew I'd be back—then vanished after Faeth.

I followed Faeth and her scattered particles, over space and a split second of time. We reappeared on a lawn somewhere out in the suburbs. Ellicott City, I figured. At least that's where Ginger said she was going to buy Sam a house. Her special, precious baby. My other sister-queens were there, waiting in darkness, ass-naked, draped in diamonds. All my sister-queens, but Ginger and Camila. Omi's cloak, the invisible barrier we threw up to hide us in plain sight from humans, shrouded the whole house and yard.

"You're fucking late." Kina waved a black velvet box in the air. "Hurry up and strip."

"I was with Moreland. You could have joined us, you know. She always likes it when you come around."

"Oh, I know she does. Tell her next time. Strip." Kina was my partner in crime. I got into the most trouble with her, but somehow I only seemed to get caught. Probably 'cause she didn't have any issues with being on time for Ginger's bullshit.

I pulled off my shirt and tossed it in the bushes. "Is Ginger fucking late too? Where's she at? This is her shindig."

"She's inside with Sam. They wanted to do the unbinding in private," Omi said.

My eyes couldn't roll hard enough. Five years ago, Ginger and Samantha couldn't even stand to be in the same room together. But then Sam's boyfriend almost murdered Ginger, and Camila wigged-out and made her a vampire instead of letting the rest of us heal her, and then Ginger needed a feeder. Long story short, Sam volunteered to feed Ginger and the blood bond made them the bestest of friends who completely forgot that they wanted to street fight each other with their Ticonderoga No. 2s in between classes.

I focused for a second until I sensed Ginger and several others milling around inside the house. We *all* felt it the moment the unbinding was complete. Sam wasn't mine, but her connection to Ginger, my sister and my queen, meant that all her feeders were in my blood, in our blood. I exhaled lightly as Samantha slipped away, then dug my nails into my palm to distract from the pain. The blood made everything clearer, made everything more intense, made everything worse.

I tried, again, not to think of how ridiculous this all was, turning a perfectly healthy, twentysomething into a vampire just because. As I ditched my jeans for my ceremonial jewels, I tried not to think about how terribly rushed of an operation this whole shit show was. Just as I finished securing the chain around my hips, Camila appeared on the lawn.

"We're ready. Please follow me."

We got in our usual line of ceremony. Camila led Kina, who led Natasha, who led Omi. I followed with Faeth behind me, the strength of our blood, the powers of our makers determining who called the shots and commanded respect.

Camila marched us right through the front door. The scene was familiar. The furniture in the open concept living/dining space had been pushed back to make room for a large table draped in a white cloth. If we did our job right, not even a single drop of blood would mar the pristine fabric.

The table itself was surrounded by all the necessary players. Sam's father and his lover, both vampires. Omi's wife, Mary. Also a vampire. And Virginia, Estella, Loni, DeeDee. Vampire, vampire, vampire, and vampire; carefully selected by our Master to help complete the ceremony. A group of demon-made beings whose blood would fill Samantha's veins with enough power to make her a bloodthirsty, immortal, shape-shifting telepath, but not strong enough that even I couldn't beat her ass if the situation called for it. An upgrade with conditions, for sure.

The only humans in the room, and the only people I was happy to see, were Amy and Danni, old feeders of Camila's who'd offered hours of entertainment when they lived in the ABO house. I would've snatched them both up for myself if Camila hadn't had first dibs.

I waved a little hello since the room was all tense and somber because we were about to drain a twenty-three-year-old girl of every drop of blood in her body, but Amy squealed her hello and Danni waved back. If they weren't there to serve a very specific purpose, I would have asked them if they wanted to party afterward.

Cleo was there too.

I didn't have many ex-lovers. I had current lovers and lovers I hadn't slept with in a while. And dead lovers. Cleo and I had

had more than our fair share of fun. So much fun it was hard to pretend that Moreland was filling her Mistress shoes, even harder to pretend that I didn't miss her. But Cleo was like ultra married, and to a human, who just happened to be our Master's daughter. And they had a kid. Yeah, ex was definitely the proper title. She looked at me, her expression neutral.

Filling in for Dalhem? I asked over the telepathic link that connected us all.

Yeah, she replied with a slight nod. *Some shit came up.*

Then she cut me off. She had some of my blood in her since I'd been there to help with her rebirth, but she had Camila's blood in her too. I couldn't override that.

Once we took our places around the table, Ginger led Samantha into the room. Sam was naked, but she had a robe on, which made sense since her dad was there. I could smell both their tears, though Sam's red-rimmed eyes were clearly obvious.

Ginger helped Sam onto the table before she addressed us all. Camila and Dalhem had helped her rehearse, I was sure.

"We come together this evening to guide our sister and friend, Samantha Grace Phillips, through her rebirth. Samantha understands the monumental weight and permanence of her decision and your presence here tonight affirms your pledge to assist Samantha, and those from which she feeds, as she becomes acclimated to this new life. Samantha, do you have anything you wish to say before we begin?"

I glanced down, waiting for her response and noticed how sobered her features had become. She was ready, even if it was still a terrible idea.

"Nope. Let's do this."

Ginger smirked. That was the Sam we all knew. Blunt and to the fucking point.

"Very well. Is there anyone among us with any words for Samantha?"

"Speak now 'cause we can't undead her," I threw out. That got a few chuckles. Mostly from Amy. Camila and Ginger both glared at me 'cause they had to do everything as a couple. "I'm kidding. God."

Of course I felt a little bad when Sam's dad started sniffling. "I just want to say I love you, sweetheart."

"Thanks, Dad," Sam mumbled back. They had their own issues.

Ginger nodded with a tight smile before she continued. "Our Master—with our Master's blessing, we shall begin."

I wanted to say something along the lines of "Let's eat," but I could tell Ginger was about to fight me so I kept my mouth shut and took my place at Sam's right thigh. Omi stood beside me, cradling Sam's tanned wrist in her palm. Kina would take her neck and Natasha her other wrist. It was overkill. One of us could have drained her in no time, but usually the heart stopped before the human was completely empty. And then there's the fact that a whole human worth of blood at once could lead to blood sickness if you weren't careful, and this way was faster and safer for Sam.

There was a pause. I caught Faeth's eyes across the table. I could hear her heart thud an extra beat ahead until it matched mine. We leaned forward together and moved the black satin covering Sam's body, shifting it just high enough to keep it from obstructing the artery. Then Ginger told us to begin.

Faeth practically dove in, all fast and hot. I had to duck a little to the left to keep our foreheads from smacking together. My fangs sliced into Samantha's skin with ease and blood flowed into my mouth. I couldn't describe the taste. It wasn't a flavor or even an aroma. It was life itself. Pleasure. Release. Growth. Awakening.

Samantha came immediately, jerking in our grasp. But we had her, holding her legs down to keep her from flopping on the table, and cutting herself on our fangs. Not a drop was to be wasted. Her moans filled the room though. The smell of her juices filled my nose. Her wet pussy was only inches from my face.

The flow continued to a trickle, a final taste.

Then Cleo called it.

"She's done."

I'd lost myself somehow to the haze, it was so much at once, but I knew I had to close the wounds and step away. Sam's heart had stopped. She lay still, her tan skin starting to take on a pasty yellow hue. Death had her, but not completely. Cleo quickly surveyed the tablecloth. It was clean. Then she instructed Mary to continue.

Mary gently took Samantha by the back of her head and chin and opened her mouth. Virginia stepped forward, dagger ready, and slit her wrist.

Ginger flinched.

I watched for a moment as blood practically poured down Sam's throat. She took some from Loni next, but it wasn't until Deedee stepped up that Samantha's heart started up again. Her lips closed lightly on Deedee's wrist, and she was feeding completely on her own by the time it was Estella's turn to top her off. Instinctively, she sealed Estella's wound, then opened her eyes.

We all braced ourselves. We were created from demons after all. These things could go wrong.

She blinked and then squinted against the bright lights in the room. She tested her fangs with the tip of her tongue. Sam was agitated, but more so by the audience than the hunger that I knew had to be clawing at her stomach. She turned to her dad first.

"I'll call you tomorrow. You can go."

No fucking clue why the man hesitated (or even why he showed up). All that was on Sam's mind was feeding from Amy and Danni, and then all that would be on her mind after that was fucking Amy and Danni. Her father and his lover didn't need to stay.

"We'll all go," Omi suggested. I didn't wait for a second cue. I kissed Sam on her cheek, welcomed her to the family, and then I was gone.

❖

My pixie dust particles didn't even make it back to the waterfront before Camila was in my head, reprimanding me like I was a teenager.

Back to the house now. We need to speak to all of you.

I changed course and appeared back in our Highness's royal apartment. Kina was already there, jeans on, pulling a T-shirt over her head. The rest, but Ginger and Camila, followed a half-second later, and started shedding their diamond adornments the moment they hit the carpet.

I joined them, until I remembered that my clothes were still in the bushes back in suburbia. "Shit."

"Here." Faeth tossed me my clothes.

"Nice. You're the best."

"Yeah."

"So, what the fuck's happening now?"

Camila was inside all of our heads a moment later, the same sense of dread filling her voice. *Don't worry. We'll keep this brief.* She joined us too, Ginger at her side.

"We know you have important places to be," Ginger said.

"Or just fuckin' to do. I mean I'm up to my eyeballs in Samantha blood. I'm pretty sure I'm not the only one who wants to sweat some of this out," I said.

"Well, I *will* keep this brief then. Your clit has places to be. A few days ago, there was an incident down at Texas U. One of Mary-Anne's feeders was kidnapped. She was snatched right before sundown, so they were able to find her quickly, but she wasn't okay.

"Of course she wasn't. She was kidnapped," I said.

"And possessed."

"What?" Kina asked, shocked enough for the rest of us.

"When they found her, a demon had a hold of her and they had to perform an exorcism."

"But that's—How?"

I didn't understand why Kina was so confused. A demonic presence got a hold of her. They kicked it out. Party over.

"The exorcism almost killed her," Ginger explained. "This wasn't some piddly weak demon their girls summoned with a Ouija board. This demon was trying to stay."

"And they have no idea who took her?" Omi asked. I could tell she was already formulating a plan. Though these girls weren't ours, and if the vampires at TU couldn't figure it out, that meant it was a Dalhem problem, not a sister-queens of ABO problem...soooooo I didn't really understand why we were still talking and not fucking.

"They couldn't track a human scent. Since they got Jessi back a few of the other girls in the Kappa chapter say that they feel like they're being followed."

"So we're packing up the Mystery Machine and heading down Texas way?" I asked.

"No. Dalhem has sent a few extra vampires down to keep an eye on things, and we've gotten some help from adult feeders in the area. But Dalhem has asked that we start being a little more vigilant while he tries to get to the bottom of this. Our blood bond is powerful enough to know when something is wrong, but I think we've all become a little lax when it comes to really paying attention to their comings and goings. I—"

"Isn't that the point though? We're not supposed to follow them around. They feed us, they live their lives, 'cause the plan and all th—"

"Tokyo, Jesus. Will you shut up for one second," Ginger snapped at me.

"What the fuck is your problem?" I responded on instinct, my growl coupled with my words.

"Red—" Camila tried to intervene, but it was too late. Her wife was all fired up for no fucking reason.

"No," Ginger said. "I was gonna save this for later, but we're gonna talk about it now. You knew how important tonight was. You knew exactly what I needed you to do. You knew exactly what time you had to be there, and you knew exactly how long it was to take, and what Sam was going to need after and you *fucking* agreed."

"Don't do that. Don't act like we have a choice. Like I can say no to you or your highness," I said to Camila 'cause really this was all her fault.

"You did have a choice, Tokyo. And you accepted," Camila replied. There was so much I could say to her, but I didn't. Not like I had the floor or anything because Ginger dug right back in.

"Dalhem gave you a choice to join this nest and watch these girls and give them everything they need. You made a pledge to them and a pledge to us. Do you have a problem with that all of a sudden?"

It didn't matter what I said. At the end of the day, Ginger was more powerful than me. I could try to fight her on this, but I would lose. So I had to take her talking to me like I was a fucking child even though I was over one hundred years older than her. I had to listen to her embarrass me in front of Faeth, Natasha, and Kina, my actual friends, 'cause even though I wanted to slap her in her stupid face it would get me nowhere, but under our Master's scaly heel.

I dug my fangs into the inside of my lip. It was the only way to keep my mouth shut, but still that only worked for a second. "I don't fucking like you."

"I don't like you either right now. I need someone to volunteer to stay near the house until this situation clears up. So why don't you go first? Maybe if you actually spend more than the thirty minutes a week it takes you to fuck and feed from the girls actually in the house, you might be reminded of just how important they are to us and how important we are to them. Go. Do bed checks."

"Fine."

"But put on some clothes first. None of the girls need to wake up and see you standing naked—"

Before she could finish, I vanished to my rooms. Before any of my sister-queens could see the hot blue tears streaming down my face.

CHAPTER THREE

Jill

When things quieted down, I made my way up to my room. Portia, my roommate, was there, talking to her boyfriend on video chat. She hated having me around during their virtual coitus, and I hated hearing it when I was trying to sleep so I made my way to the study lounge. Next year, I'd have to make chapter vice president at least to get my own room. I'd have to play up my administrative skills to even get nominated, but something had to be done. I needed my own space. I'd thought about dropping a major and possibly graduating early, but I wanted these degrees, and I wanted to see things with Alpha Beta Omega, the institution, through. Even if I could live without its members.

I knocked out my homework, but the focus was still there and Portia was still awake. I thought about texting my best friend, James, but when I saw the time on my phone I knew he was asleep. On top of choosing to serve the brother-kings of Omega Beta Alpha, he was the star player on our university's football team. Practice was enough to wear him out. Frat activities and feeding his vampire had him in bed hours before me every night. I pulled out my presentation online for my Human Sexuality class. If Dr. Miller didn't get me the help that I needed there was a possibility I'd have to rework the entire scope of the project.

I looked at the assignment sheet. And then I realized I wasn't alone. Our sister-queens all had their own scents. Light and faint to humans, apparently, but I realized that if you were actually paying attention, it was easy to pick them out. I made it a point to recognize their unique perfumes. I smelled citrus. Tokyo was lurking in the door. Not saying anything.

"It's rude to stare," I said. "You probably know that."

"Calm down. I'm just observing. You're the only one up."

"Portia's asleep?"

"Yup. Put her laptop up and tucked her in myself."

I glanced up from my computer screen. Tokyo didn't have any pants on, just a black T-shirt and a really small pair of underwear. Typical Tokyo. It was like she was allergic to clothes. "That's sweet of you."

"You got a lot of homework?" She came over and stood behind me. I swear these vampires knew nothing about privacy and personal space.

"Yeah. That's why I'm the only one up because this is usually the only time I can get any quiet." I paused a moment, hoping she would take the hint and leave me alone. I just needed to handle twenty more minutes of tinkering and then I was going to try to get some sleep. But that would have been too easy. Tokyo picked up the assignment sheet.

"Oh, you have Miller?"

"Yeah."

"She's good."

"If you say so."

"A bunch of my girls have taken her courses. They loved her."

"Yeah, well, she's not for everyone."

"You got her Monday, Wednesday, Friday at least. Shorter periods."

"Yeah."

"You're doing a double major, huh? Is that you or your dads? They want you to live the dream, be the dream, chase the dream? The quadrilingual OBGYN, out to save the world one set of sex organs at a time."

Maybe it was late and I was just tired and cranky and already had things in the week ahead waiting for me, but it was only Monday, and I was not in the mood to have even part of this conversation, especially not with someone like Tokyo.

"I know you guys know all these things about us, but this is the first time you've spoken to me beyond hello in practically three years. Usually when you speak to someone for the first time, it's polite to let them tell you about themselves."

I expected a comeback. Something, but when I looked up she was just looking down at my assignment sheet. Whatever she was about to say seemed to evaporate in her mouth. She shrugged and then smiled her usual casual smile. Nothing bothered Tokyo. She put my assignment sheet on the table with a little pat.

"You're right. Good luck on your project."

"Thank you." Now please leave.

"Does Ginger know you're up?"

"I suppose she does. I'm up this late every night."

"Yeah, you—"

I spun around and looked up at her. "I what?"

"Nothing. Don't stay up too late. Ginger'll freak. Or Camila will on her behalf."

I snorted a bit. That was pretty funny. "Night, Tokyo," I said, but when I looked up again she was gone.

❖

As soon as the bell went off, I grabbed my things and marched to the front of the lecture hall. Two days, and Dr. Miller had yet to respond to my e-mail. But I was done being ignored.

Either she was going to take my request seriously or I was going to hand in a fraction of the assignment.

I had to wait for two students to finish their quick conversations with Dr. Miller, but I eventually got my turn. I glanced at the girl standing to her left, letting her know I was next. I felt a little bad when she smiled at me. Not bad enough to let her cut though.

"Miss Babineux. Just the person I wanted to speak with."

"I assume you got my e-mail?"

"I did and I found you a partner. With a few caveats."

"And those would be?"

"I will be grading your presentation for this class and this class only, but I will recommend to the chancellor's office that they send someone over to see your presentation to evaluate its merits as a university program."

"And what else?"

"If you send me one more e-mail like that, demanding that I bend to your personal ambitions, I'm failing you or having you removed from my class. It's that simple."

I wasn't entirely sure Dr. Miller actually had the power to do that, over one e-mail no less, but I didn't want to argue with her. I needed that class for my first major and I needed the A I was going to get in that class to ensure my place on the dean's list.

"Miss Dryer registered late and is a little behind. I'm letting her assist you to make up for missing the first quiz. Plus, what you've outlined sounds so fascinating, I'm sure you'll both enjoy the A."

"Hi," the other girl said cheerfully and then she held out her hand. "I'm Brayley."

I shook it. This wasn't her fault. "Nice to meet you."

"Fast friends already. See you Friday!" I glanced at the back of Dr. Miller's head for a second as she practically skipped out of the classroom. She was the last to go, leaving us to ourselves.

"Looks like we're partners." I took a moment to really look at Brayley as she spoke. She was white. Average build, smallish breasts. Taller than me, like most everybody. She had brown hair cut up in an asymmetrical bob. It was a cute style, but beyond that she wasn't very pretty. Her face was too dull for her haircut, and her lips were too thin for the amount and shade of lipstick she had on. The sparkly dark pink wasn't working for her. And her mascara was clumping together. When I thought about it, she wasn't unattractive. Her makeup just sucked. She seemed a little overdressed in an MU hoodie considering it was really hot for the beginning of October, but maybe she ran cold.

"Did she tell you about my project?" I asked.

"You plan to come up with a multi-part, comprehensive, intersectional sex education program that you're hoping the university will offer for incoming students?"

"Correct. Are you up for that?"

"Yeah, definitely. I think it's a great idea."

"Why were you late this semester?"

"I was busy giving my unwanted baby up for adoption. I got my trichomoniasis cleared up while I was at it. If only I'd had a comprehensive sex ed class when I was a freshman."

"Not funny."

"I thought it was. My grandpa died suddenly and I wanted to be there for my mom."

"Oh. I'm sorry to hear that."

"Him and I weren't really close," she said with a bit of an odd shrug.

"Well, I hope you're ready to get started."

"It's not due until the end of the semester. We have time."

I looked at her for a moment and then turned and started walking for the door. I didn't have time to wait for yet another person to take me seriously.

"Jill. Wait."

I whipped around to face her again and she almost ran into me. "Have you looked at the syllabus for this class? It's an advanced human sexuality course and she's not covering disease or reproduction. Everyone in the room is going to come up with different variations on women's sexual liberation and the mating rituals of cavemen. Perhaps, maybe one brave person will tackle the complexities of gender. I want to cover all that and more, things that are affecting us now. This grade and this presentation are important to me. If you want to help we're starting tonight."

"I like your accent. Where are you from?"

"Ugh, you're serious. Montreal."

"Oh, cool."

"Yes, it is fascinating."

Brayley laughed then slapped me on the arm. "Tonight at the library, seven?"

"That works fine. I'll see you then." Hopefully, Brayley would pull her weight. If not, she wouldn't be sharing in the grade. It was that simple. We both walked out of the lecture hall. I had to use the restroom, but when she turned in that same direction, I headed for the front door. I wasn't in the mood for any more awkward small talk.

James was waiting for me outside on the steps. "How'd it go? What did Dr. Miller say?"

"Fine," I grumbled, just as Brayley walked by.

"Seven," she said. "I'll be on time."

I nodded and gave her a tight smile.

"Who was that?" James asked.

"My new partner."

He laughed and nudged my shoulder as we started walking toward the cafeteria. "What's the problem? I thought you wanted help. I thought you demanded it."

"Yeah, I do. I guess I should have been more specific. Where's Van?"

"He's meeting us." Our friend Van had a crush on James. I thought they were acting on it, but there were all sorts of conditions. Van's parents were very conservative and expected him to marry an Indian girl. He wasn't ready to tell them he was gay. And James wasn't ready to tell his coaches and his teammates or any potential NFL scouts that he was gay.

"How are things going there?" I asked.

"I don't know what you're talking about."

"Okay." I didn't have to pressure James for details. We were both bad at keeping secrets from each other.

"He stayed in my room last night."

"And?"

"And I don't know what I'm doing."

"I wish I could give you some advice." We both laughed then.

"Yeah, I don't know. What's that saying? Those who can't do teach. Maybe those who can't do shouldn't teach those who can't do either and refuse to learn."

"When I'm ready, maybe you can give me some pointers. At least you have someone who wants to spend the night in your bed."

"We had sex," he blurted out.

"I figured."

"I need to just follow your plan. School. Football. Feeding and fucking the undead. No time for anything else."

"It's not a bad plan. It'll keep you busy." So busy you didn't want to have time for anything else.

CHAPTER FOUR

Tokyo
Unjust House Arrest Day 3

I'd spent the last forty-eight hours in a miserable cycle. Daylight in my avian form, flying all over campus, keeping an eye on the girls. Nighttime, stuck in the house keeping an eye on the girls. One of Camila's feeders, Beth, totally had an admirer that was a hair away from being a stalker, but as far as I could tell, the girls were perfectly safe. And I was bored out of my fucking mind.

There had been no more attempts on any of the feeders at Texas U. Jessi was recovering just fine, though I'm sure Mary-Anne was worried as shit. Still, there had been no evil demon sightings, no strange behavior, no surprises. Nothing the slightest bit exciting to make my punishment feel at least a little worthwhile. I got it. A feeder being kidnapped and possessed was real fucking bad, but we were talking about a one-time thing. I needed a fucking break.

Moreland humored me via text for a whole hour before she abandoned me for Luke and Krystal. I couldn't blame her. Her pets were fun and limber. I checked up on Ansley and Juniper, my only feeders outside of the house, whom Ginger kindly agreed to let me visit once a week for thirty minutes until she decided I'd learned whatever stupid fucking lesson she was trying to teach me.

I even did the rounds with my makers, who I rarely checked in with unless it was a special occasion or that weird homesickness that came calling from time to time clawed at my neck. Hattie, my primary maker, whose powerful blood gave me my rank amongst my sister-queens, was glad to hear from me, but didn't waste a fucking second chewing me out when she found out that I'd gotten in trouble. Again. That put an end to my "calls home."

I'd sat in on the girls' weekly chapter meeting, run by one of my girls. I was proud of Chelsea for getting elected to chapter president, but fuck, were those meetings boring. Same shit as always. Community service on Saturday morning, pick a song for the homecoming lip sync battle, get started planning group costumes for Halloween, some frat was having a party, should they go. Twice a week, the girls had this thing called sister counseling where they could vent their troubles to two members of the sorority and it would be kept in confidence, but only kinda 'cause they still spilled all the relevant beans to Ginger and Camila as soon as the sessions were over. So there were reminders for that.

The whole time, I just sat there in the corner, resisting the urge to stab myself in the eye. After the meeting, I pulled my youngest baby, Yazmeen, aside for a quick feeding and a dry hump, but she had a paper to write so I couldn't keep her long.

We had every channel imaginable, and *everything* I tried was horrible. Or a repeat. And that was why I always went out. *People* were fun to play with. I needed people to entertain me. So if I couldn't bother the girls, and my sister-queens and I were sick of looking at each other, I went out. It wasn't fair really. Kina went with me most of the time, and she didn't get blasted for being away from the house or not caring about the girls' well-being. She'd ditched me already, in fact, taken off to our favorite strip club with Natasha and her husband, Rodrick, who were usually always down to tie me up and spank me around when Moreland was busy, but they were at the strip club with Kina!

Driven insane by the walls of my own underground apartment/prison of boredom and doom, I found Faeth where I knew she'd be on a Wednesday night. Right on her couch, half watching her TV. The original *Point Break* was on, but she wasn't paying attention. Instead, she was absently tuning her already tuned guitar. The stupid thing hadn't been out of tune the whole ten years I'd known her. I flopped down beside her and tried to get into the movie, but I couldn't. Too fucking boring.

"How can you stand this?" I asked as I slid to the floor. Her carpet needed to be cleaned.

"Stand what?"

"Just sitting here. Surely that guitar is not that interesting?"

"It is. Gives me something to do with my hands, but I'm in my head too, yeah? Taylor's birthday is next week." Faeth tapped herself on the temple. "I'm planning her birthday party."

"Highlight of your life, huh? A nineteen-year-old's birthday party?"

"I don't know what you want me to say. This is where I want to be."

"Then why didn't you volunteer for this bullshit, keeping close to the girls in case of accidental kidnapping? I mean you practically never leave the house unless Kina and I drag you out or if the Highnesses need you for an errand."

"Don't forget all the spying I do on the girls."

"And there's that." Faeth had joined me the last two days in bird form. Forty-two girls were a lot to keep track of. "You live for this shit. Why do I have to stay in?"

"Because you couldn't keep your mouth shut, yeah?"

"Whatever. Was I wrong though?"

Faeth shrugged.

"This neutral bit isn't going to work for you forever."

"You were both right. How about that?"

"I said whatever."

"What time is it?" Faeth asked, changing the subject.

I glanced at the clock on her DVR box. "One a.m."

"Go do a bed check. Gives you a chance to stretch your legs, yeah?"

I would have snapped if Faeth hadn't shot me her signature smile. She was such a big oaf. In her natural form she was tall, and the years she'd spent on her father's sheep farm in New Zealand had shaped her into somewhat of a muscled beast. But she was so beautiful, and such a young, innocent vampire, it was hard not to love her. And it was hard to keep from trying to corrupt her at every turn. Our baby vampire sister.

"I'm gonna choke you." I said, finally.

"Where do you want to be?"

"Nowhere, just not here."

"You're ungrateful. That's the problem."

"For what? This?" I waved my hands up and down my body.

"Mhmm."

"Whatever. I'm going to check beds. Wanna fuck when I get back?"

Faeth's hands stilled a moment and she cocked her head to the side. "Hmmmeh," she said with another shrug. "Why not?"

"Sweet." Just as I was about to vanish, Kina appeared on the other side of the door. She knocked out of courtesy.

"Come in, yeah?" Faeth yelled.

Kina vanished through the door. She felt all kinds of off.

"What's wrong with you?" I asked.

She flopped down in the chair beside me. "Nothing. I'm just thinking about Mary-Anne's girl."

"Did you find anything out?" I asked.

"No."

"Have you seen anything like this before?"

Being born and turned in the sixteen hundreds gave Kina a whole lot of mileage. "Yes and no. Shit, I feel like I should draw a diagram. There are these different planes and we're here on Earth, in our galaxy in the middle, for the sake of this argument. Usually, when something crosses the planes it's random. Or it's undead like us and it's never gone between to begin with. Unless."

"Unless what?" I asked, but I felt Faeth put down her guitar between us. She leaned forward.

"Unless it's planned. I don't know, I would feel better if this was a random possession and exorcism. Evil has toyed with humans forever, but this feels orchestrated. It kidnapped her."

Kina had a point. I'd heard of a few incidents over time, but usually it had to do with evil being invited accidentally or a human stumbling into the wrong place at the wrong time. Those possessions had been more of a desperate grab. A kidnapping changed things.

"What can we do?" Faeth asked.

"Nothing. I tried to speak with our Master just now, but he said what Ginger said. Keep our eyes open and watch over the girls. I'm sure he's spoken to Paneo about it. This is definitely more her area of expertise." Dalhem's demon-sister had global reign over all six demon-masters and their blood-bound children. There wasn't much we could do without their command.

"I'm sure they'll get to the bottom of this," I said as I reached over and gave her knee a squeeze. "I'm going to do bed checks, then Faeth and I are gonna play hide the dildo. You want in?"

"Actually, I came to see if Faeth wanted to go to Tens. Carmen is back from moving her mom. I promised I'd throw a wad of cash her way when she was back in town."

Faeth jumped up. "I'm in. Let's go."

"What! What the fuck? You're both going to ditch me?"

Kina stood, then leaned over and kissed me soundly on the mouth. "Yup. See you later." Then she was gone.

I shook a bit as Faeth slapped me on the back with her massive hand. "We'll play your dirty game later." She stuck her tongue out the side of her mouth and made an obscene gesture with her hands before leaving me alone on her floor like an asshole.

❖

I vanished up to the kitchen and found the first floor nearly empty. I followed the sound of a TV into the living room and saw one of Natasha's sophomores, Rayna, was passed out on the couch, still in her clothes. I cut off the infomercials and carried her upstairs. All the girls were accounted for; all but three were asleep. One of Omi's juniors, Kait, and Lydia, the freshman she was hooking up with, were up watching Netflix.

And then there was Jill.

The light in the study lounge was on and there she was, her notes and books splayed out on the table. There was no reason for me to talk to her. She was alive and accounted for. Ginger would be ecstatic. Plus, Jill had made it pretty clear that she didn't want anyone to talk to her while she was studying.

I cloaked myself and stood there, watching her as she looked back and forth between her notebook and her laptop.

Jill had never had many friends. That small fact had been in her dossier when she'd pledged. One real friend in high school and really only one friend now. One of the OBA boys, Jim Fa'u, had latched on to her their freshman year. When he wasn't busy with his twin brother Tim, football, or his own fraternity responsibilities, they seemed to be attached at the hip. But as far as we knew, he was it. That's why Ginger had picked her. She felt bad for the misunderstood, unpopular types. And when we found out how annoying Jill was, we'd all been retroactively grateful that we hadn't gotten stuck with her.

But over the years, Jill had changed. She was still four feet tall with a fifteen-foot mouth. And it was impossible to take her seriously because of that adorable French Canadian accent, but looking at her then and thinking over the last two and a half years, there were definitely some differences in tiny Jill Babineux.

For one, she'd gotten her braces off, and practically none of the girls in the house called her Jaws anymore. Just a few seniors and juniors, out of habit. She used to cry on a dime, but she seemed to have fixed that. She was still a stickler for rules and procedure, but thanks to her, the girls had won chapter of the year for community outreach and service. As the chapter's Wellness chairperson, she'd suggested that the girls vote on who should lead sister counseling, instead of letting the chapter president and vice president automatically fill those roles. The switch led to the girls being more open with the sisters they chose to talk with. So far, Carrie and D'Monique had done a good job.

She'd done a lot of good for the chapter and herself, I suppose. Her grades were excellent, she was cute, but she was still Jill.

"I don't know which one of you is there, but I can feel you watching me." She didn't look up when she spoke, but in the next second, she launched a pencil in my direction. I snatched it mid flight, then vanished across the hall and into the room beside her. Just a little tap on the shoulder made her jump.

"Oh my God! Don't do that!" She whipped around toward me, all pink in her light brown cheeks and furious.

"How'd you know I was there?"

"That trick you do just makes you all invisible, but matter is still matter, and it gives off energy and takes up space."

"Ginger always did like 'em smart. Whatcha working on?" I asked, taking a seat on the table.

"You know, that chair would be more suitable. Considering you're not wearing any pants."

"Yeah, I am." I hiked up the oversized shirt I had on to show her the shorts I was wearing. They were small, but they were there.

"I guess."

"Still working on your project?" Her notebook was opened to a page covered with furiously scribbled writing that was divided into two columns. I scanned the page and caught things on various issues of sexual health and where they might find possible speakers to handle each topic. One column header said *Jill* and the other said *Brayley*. "And you got yourself a partner!"

"Is there a reason for your sudden interest in me and my academic life?"

"Not really. You're up. I'm up. I was just curious. That's all. Question though. How are you so sure of the direction of all this sex ed stuff if you've never had sex?"

She got even pinker. "I have too had sex!"

"Hmmm, have you though? And I'm not talking about vampire related sex. I mean caught up in a moment, first crush, can't keep your hands off each other, or drunken mistake out past curfew sex."

"Have you?! I mean isn't *all* the sex you have vampire related?"

"I—huh, that's a good call. I kinda have. The stuff before I was turned is really fuzzy, but I've been in love since and I've had sex with people I wasn't blood bound to, but I've been a vampire for a long time."

"How old are you?" she asked with this look and tone of suspicion like she expected me to lie.

"Ahhh, hundred and fifty-one. Give or take a few years. Not as old as Kina, not as young as Ginger. You know." I wiggled my fingers in the air for emphasis.

"Oh, well, I don't see what my sex life has to do with organizing informational sessions. You don't have to be a murderer to be an FBI profiler."

"True, but you have to get inside the head of a killer. You go to crime scenes. And look, this is exactly what I'm talking about. You've outlined a program on birth control, STDs, and general reproductive health. Do you see anything missing?" I turned the sheet so Jill could look at it again.

"I think we've got everything covered."

"Exactly. This is what matters to you, but what about a talk on healthy relationships? Sexual orientation and sexual expression. You're dealing with college students and you have nothing on here about rape and other sexual violence. You could do ten seminars on sex and gender and race alone.

"I don't see anything that addresses the needs of your transgender classmates. What about Taylor? Wouldn't you want her to feel included? And then there's sex and disability. You're missing the joys of sex, the joys of masturbation, safe toy play. You're taking such a clinical approach you're ignoring the real concerns of your target audience.

"You run your programs this way and you might as well just add another standard biology class to the course curriculum. A good PR blitz might get your first run of seats filled, but I doubt you'll have any repeat customers. People want to talk these sorts of things out in a safe, open environment. They don't want a lecture."

"I didn't think of it that way."

"'Cause you're not having sex?"

"I don't think it's that simple."

"Maybe not, but there's something to be said about experience and how it correlates with empathy. So maybe you don't need to get out there and fuck, but upping your human interactions might help."

"I—"

"Anyway, I'll let you get back to it. If you want some actual experience in the porking department, let me know. I'm around."

"You mean…for us. To have sex."

"Ah, yeah. We're not blood bound, so technically it wouldn't be vampire related."

"I—um, I'll think about it."

"Sounds good. Later." I hopped off the table and left her to her work.

As I walked back downstairs, I started thinking more seriously on the offer I'd just made Jill. She *was* cute. It could be fun. And even though we had some pretty firm rules making it pretty damn clear that we couldn't drink from each other's feeders, there was absolutely no rule against sleeping with them. Like I said, could be fun.

CHAPTER FIVE

Jill

I took the night to sleep on the interesting suggestions Tokyo had made. She was wrong about a few things. I'd lost my virginity freshman year, to Ginger during our first feeding. That counted. And I'd fooled around with Skylar, Carrie, Hollis, Emma, and Tara in the time we'd served Ginger. Yes, our run-ins had always been during our Friday Night Movie feeding, but it still counted. Another girl's head between your legs counted. Your mouth on another girl's breast while another girl climaxed on your thigh counted. And even Ginger didn't know it, but James and I had had sex too.

We both wanted to know what it was like to have sex outside of the feedings, so we tried it once. It was okay. Our difference in size made the whole thing practically silly, but we both figured some things out, like that we didn't really want to sleep with each other again and that we both preferred the company of our own sex. So yes, I had completely had sex before, but what Tokyo said about the wanting, urgency, the heat? I'd never felt that before. Perhaps maybe once.

There was my sorority sister, Benny. She was a senior when I was a freshman, and now she was married, to Tokyo's ex-lover to make things more ridiculous. I would be lying if I said I didn't think I loved Benny once upon a time, but after she left with Cleo and they started their family, I saw what *they* had was love and what I felt was admiration and lust. I looked up to Benny, and I wanted her to like me maybe because I didn't love myself completely. But that was then.

Now I knew what came first—school. And the rest could definitely wait. College romances were just as fleeting as high school affairs. I only knew of one human couple who had survived Alpha Beta Omega, and even then, Amy and Danni hadn't gotten all the way out. They still provided blood to vampires outside of the house. That was not the kind of long-term adult relationship I was waiting for.

I was waiting for something different, something special, which isn't cliché at all, because why would I want something that everyone else had? I was waiting for certainty. Permanence. Someone who knew herself as well as I knew myself. Someone not bound to an immortal blood-drinking demoness. Someone who was mine and mine only. I wasn't going to find that person under the ABO roof or at Maryland University, period. And I certainly wasn't going to find that type of connection in the much frequented bed of Tokyo herself. There was no difference in the convenient encounters I had shared with my sorority sisters and the emotionless sex I'd find in Tokyo's temporary, conditional company.

But she did have a point. I had to think about my audience. I was dealing with hormonal college students who leapt before they looked and had the morning afters and the confused, failed relationships to prove it, if the girls I lived with served as a reliable control group. I had to get this right.

The next time I met Brayley, I brought up the idea of changing our approach.

"Are you sexually active?" I asked her as soon as she sat at our table in the library.

She hesitated a moment, probably because James and our other fraternity brother, Van, were there. But James and Van didn't care about our presentation in the slightest. They'd tagged along to our first two meetings and had completely ignored us. Except for when James interrupted to show me the drawing he was tooling with.

"I—yeah. Why?"

I brought up the changes Tokyo had mentioned. "I want your perspective. What do you think is important?"

"Well, what about what *you* think is important? You're asking me like I'm the sexual expert. I take it you're not…climbing the smoke pole."

"I'm not attracted to guys, but no, I'm not…climbing anything or its equivalent."

"Oh. Well, that doesn't mean you don't have opinions or have things you're curious about."

"I do, but I don't want this to be about me."

"Oh, come on. Yes, you do or you wouldn't be this anal about something that's not due for another eight weeks and makes up like a sixteenth of our grade. What about you guys? What programs do you think you and other frat dudes would want to see?" she asked James and Van.

"Gay athletes," James said. "I want a program about how being gay in professional sports is actually very common and how being gay doesn't make you any less of a man or an athlete." He and his brother had been discussing whether or not James should come out to NFL scouts.

"Are all three of you gay?" Brayley asked.

"Yes," we all answered.

"So the rumors are true," Brayley said with a smile.

"About ABO and OBA being queer friendly Greek organizations?" I clarified. "Yes."

"Why don't you guys survey a few people? Hit some of the freshman dorms? The other Greeks, and just ask? Some people are bound to take you seriously and then you get some actual direction from your constituents," Van said.

"What's wrong?" Brayley asked as she looked in my direction. "I think that's a great idea. And we have the time."

"No, you're right. And you're right too, Van. That's a great idea. I'm just thinking." I hated to delete my whole outline and the progress we made, but I selected the key parts of the document on my laptop screen in front of me and did it anyway.

Even more, I hated that Tokyo was right.

❖

Tokyo

I'd accepted the darkness, let the bleak loneliness of isolation consume me, and soon I became resigned to the fact that I was fucking *grounded* and I had to get the approval of a fucking three-year-old vampire before I could leave the house again. I considered talking to our Master about it. His word outweighed Ginger's to the power of ten, and if he knew exactly how silly it was for me to be following the girls around nearly twenty-four seven, he'd lift Ginger's stupid punishment and let me go back to the carefree bloodsucking life I was meant to live.

But Dalhem was busy with bigger things. Ultimately, he was responsible for all of our feeders and all of us. I downplayed the severity of this situation a lot, but he was responsible for every vampire and every human we touched in this part of the world. As a full demon, his failure to protect us would have complete and eternal consequences for him. And for us. So yeah, it was a big deal if there was a chance more of our girls could get snatched up off the street. And it was a big deal if any kind of evil entity was trying to use her body, for any purpose.

I came to this realization during a *Pretty Little Liars* mini-marathon. My darling Yazmeen had the afternoon off and came by to spend it with me. I stopped paying attention after the first episode, but I sat with her, playing with her hair. Sometime after the third episode and before I sent her off to get some dinner, I considered what it would be like to lose her before her time. I had been very lucky. All of my feeders had died of old age. I'd always been there in time to save those who were sick or injured. Definitely lucky. But even feeling their pain had been fucking awful and overwhelming. What would I do if a demon, the bad kind, tried to take one of my girls from me?

I didn't feel so bad about sticking around the house anymore. Was I bored out of my fucking mind? Yes. But was I pissed? No. I wanted to be there, to fulfill my pledge. I loved my girls that much and I wanted to keep them safe. Still, I had selfishly been looking forward to our movie night. Aside from their Saturday morning charity work, the girls did what they wanted with their weekends, but Friday night, they were ours.

In our all-purpose room, a corridor down from Natasha's apartment, I collapsed on my usual couch, and my girls wasted no time crowding around me. D'Monique had had a terrible week. I knew she was ready to feed me then get a good fucking from the others. Faeth's taste in movies was awful, and it was her week to pick, so I knew for sure no one was going to pay attention to whatever she put on once everyone was settled.

Ginger always started the night off by greeting the girls, telling them some corny shit about how they made it through another week. She also loved to remind the seniors how many weeks they had to graduation. I started fingering D'Monique the moment she sat down and pulled my hand between her legs. It was nothing to pull her tiny pajama shorts and her underwear to the side. I pretended to listen to whatever Ginger was talking about. But then she waved Jill forward.

"Before we get started, Jill has an announcement and a favor to ask all of you. So please give her your attention."

"Thank you," Jill muttered.

"Jaws!" Skylar yelled from across the room. Jill ignored her, but I noticed a faint tic near her eye. The nickname still bothered her.

"Um, I have a project to do in my human sexuality class, and I want to create actual programs, or at least, generate a blueprint for actual programs, I think the university should implement. I was going in one direction, but Tokyo gave me the idea to turn things back to other students like you guys."

Ginger and Camila both flashed me looks, one hundred percent surprise. Two hundred percent suspicion. Kina and Omi started handing out pieces of paper and pens.

"If you can circle the topics that interest you and then write in one topic or issue that's not listed," Jill added.

"Can we have a program on gang bangs, like the one we should be having right now?" Yazmeen asked.

I tried to shhh her, but the comment was already out.

"If group sex is something that interests you, then please write it in."

I smiled, feeling an odd bit of pride light in my chest. It was nice to see Jill holding her own. I mean, she always had; I guess I just noticed her now. There were some more comments hurled from around the room, a few more jokes about the clap and eating ass (we'd turned these poor girls into a bunch of freaks) but after a few minutes, things around the room settled down.

There was more chatter, forty-two girls taking a sex survey called for a bit of discussion, but they seemed to be taking it seriously. Navaeh almost broke her pencil circling "Pregnancy." I looked over Chelsea's shoulder and was impressed at the variety of options Jill and her partner had added. They added all the topics we talked about, plus a few points about splitting the seminars up by gender. McKenna caught me looking as she wrote in her answer.

"I don't know. I think speed dating on campus would be fun. Get to know more people."

"Or know who you want to avoid," I replied.

She giggled. "Exactly."

Ginger and Camila collected the surveys as the girls finished up. I watched Jill as she ducked out of the room, to stash the papers I assumed. I didn't watch the archway long, because before Faeth could even fire up the action movie of choice, Chelsea was sliding into my lap and taking her shirt off, while D'Monique guided my hand back between her legs. With both their pulse points and suddenly bare tits inches from my face, it was hard to focus on anything else in the room, but when I came up for air three delicious veins later, Jill was gone.

And I noticed a couple of hours after that she had never come back.

❖

The house was quiet when I did my final head count. A bunch of girls were still downstairs with their sister-queens. I'd left Navaeh and Chelsea in my bed. When everyone was accounted for, I knew I should head back down and catch the few hours of shut-eye I needed, but something kept me on the second floor. I pulled my robe closed as I drifted back to Jill's room.

Her door was cracked. I poked my head in and saw her where I'd glanced her on my first pass, sitting on the floor surrounded by papers. Her roommate Portia was downstairs with Kina.

"Hey, how's it going?" I asked quietly

"Good." She actually stopped reading and looked up at me. And smiled. It was a little bit of a corner of the mouth sort of thing, but it was still a smile. I'd never gotten one of those out of her.

"Is it okay if I come in?"

"Yeah."

"Actually." I looked down at myself just before I sat down. I didn't have anything on under my short robe. I vanished down to my bedroom and came back in a pair of sweats and a T-shirt. This time when I joined her she wouldn't have to worry about catching a sneak peek of my labia. "There we go. Better?"

"Better."

I parked it on the carpet and picked up one of the surveys. Someone had written in *Divorce* and on another *How does the morning after pill work?*

"Did you already survey some other students? This looks like a lot more than forty-two." There had to be at least a hundred little slips of paper splayed out between us.

"James and Van got the OBA boys to fill some out before they started their game night."

"Oh. Who brought them over?"

"I ran over and got them from James."

"During the movie?"

"Yeah."

"You left the house?"

"I know it was after the nine o'clock curfew, but it was just across the street and I came right back."

"No, I know. I just—"

"I'm twenty years old. I'm allowed to cross the street alone."

"I know. I just—You dip out on movie night a lot, huh?"

She lifted one shoulder a little. "It's the same thing every week. I enjoy it, but—"

"But you know Ginger's waiting to get back to Camila? Takes a little bit of the fun out of it?"

"Yeah. And the other girls don't really like me." My flinch of shock must not have been subtle 'cause Jill caught it. "What?"

"I don't know. I guess I didn't really think about you knowing that, that you're not exactly popular with the other girls. You sound used to it. Or okay with it."

"I'm not okay with it, but I can't change my personality. Can't change my enthusiasm, honestly. That's what they don't like."

Jill was right. Annoying described her in most situations, but it was more like she was overly enthusiastic and didn't know when to dial it back. I had the same problem sometimes, but I didn't know how to turn it off.

"Some of my sister-queens don't like me either," I told her. "Ginger doesn't. Camila used to, but she doesn't anymore. And Omi just tolerates me because of our bond, but I know she can't stand me. She thinks I'm too loud."

"You are loud."

"I know."

"I can be too though."

"Not lately." Like I said, she'd changed. "Not around the house at least." We were both quiet for a while, organizing the papers into neat piles. I figured if I was going to hang out in her room any longer I should probably change the subject.

"I'm surprised you took my advice with the surveys. Any interesting results so far?"

"I thought about what you said, and I felt like you were on to something, and it looks like you're right. A lot of people wanted to know about safe sex, but a lot of the write-in issues were more about interpersonal relationships. Some questions about being asexual or aromantic. One person asked about getting married young, and there was a write-in about divorce."

"I saw. What are you taking from that?"

"A lot of us are lonely. I don't know if we need proper sex ed or a group hug."

I didn't know what to say to that. I didn't really want to think about it. I didn't like the idea of any of our girls or our boys across the street being unhappy.

"Or like this one." She handed me one of the surveys. The handwriting was so bad I knew it had to be from one of the OBA boys. *How do I know if I'm bi?* was written at the bottom. "The group hug might be a good place to start. Did you fill out one?"

"That's what I was sitting here contemplating. What I would put on the survey."

"Well, start with what you want."

"It's more complex than that. I've been thinking about the other thing you said. About being available for sex."

"Oh. Yeah. I'm sorry. I shouldn't have said that. I know that's not your style. Sometimes, my mouth—"

"No, but I was wondering if you still would."

"Have sex with you?"

"Not quite. I was hoping you'd be my girlfriend, or at least pretend to be. I want to know what it's like not to be alone. Maybe if I know what it's like to care about someone and have someone care about me, I'll have a better grasp on some of the issues the other students are facing. Empathy *is* key to science, contrary to common belief."

She wasn't mine, but at that exact second I felt every ounce of Jill's pain. Did Ginger have any idea how miserable Jill was? How badly she was hurting? My answer was almost automatic and not entirely for selfless reasons.

"I think I could swing that. Like pretend. Do you want me or just anybody? I can shape shift you know?" I added the last part, just to keep things light. The effort earned me another smile.

"That's why I thought of you. We don't really know each other and you can pick the body you inhabit. That's useful if I want to create a situation where I'm starting a new relationship with someone who is seemingly unfamiliar to me." Jill tilted her head, giving me a full once-over. "Shorter. Everyone is taller than me. For once I'd like to be face-to-face with a girl."

"Done." I snapped my fingers and shrank my form down to her four feet eleven inch proportions. I changed my face too, a face I'd used when I was younger. I was still Japanese though. I didn't like to change that. None of the girls had seen this person before. And I always liked my boobs a little on the bigger side. "How's this?"

"I like it."

"Does this person have a name?" I asked.

"Hmm, I have always liked the name Bridgette?"

"The way the French pronounce it?"

"The French do pronounce everything better. But I don't think I could call you that. Too weird."

"How about we use it as a code name?"

"Let's do that."

"Okay, now that we've got that figured out, what would your pretend girlfriend do first?"

"Help me put these papers away and then cuddle with me in bed until we both fall asleep?"

"'Kay. Let's do that." We made quick work of the papers, then climbed into her bed. It was strange being so short. The form I usually held came in at around five ten, but we both were so little we fit easily in her bed side by side. She cut off the lights, all but a little decorative nightlight near her bed. Another thing I forgot, Jill was afraid of the complete dark.

"What do we do now?"

"Since you asked me to be your boo and not your fuck buddy, maybe we should just talk. Get the new girlfriend conversation flowing."

"Do you know how to play twenty questions?" Jill suggested.

"I used to play it with James all the time."

"Refresh me."

As Jill gave me the breakdown, I reached over and grabbed her hand. She froze for a moment, maybe not sure what I was trying to do, but then our fingers laced together, and came apart. I stroked a finger along her palm and then the tips of our fingers danced against each other, tapping in rhythm. She seemed hesitant at first, but soon she took the lead, doing some tracing and tapping of her own. It was part of the game, the make-believe. That's what I told myself anyway, when my skin started to tingle. The heat in my stomach was a part of the game too. At least, that's what I told myself.

CHAPTER SIX

Jill

I fell asleep sometime during our fifth round of twenty questions. Tokyo was better at it than I was. She had a firmer grasp of pop culture and a brain that was magically wired to retain more information. She also watched more TV than I did. She mentioned shows and people, recent stuff, that I'd never heard of. But we had fun. Being with her was fun.

A series of beeps from my cell phone woke me up a few minutes before my alarm was supposed to go off. I reached for it and almost knocked over a small, clear spray bottle on my nightstand. It looked liked there were orange and lemon slices crammed inside and a sprig of something green. Botany was not on my list of course requirements.

Another text pinged my phone. The contact name made me smile. Bridgette.

Wake up. You have community service!

I sat up and sent a text back.

Good morning to you too.

What's in the bottle?

She was texting me back before I could put my phone down and get out of bed.

It's perfume.

Kinda.

It'll cover my scent. Typically, a shower would do it

But we were touching a lot. And if I keep being your girlfriend...

I replied.

I'll have your scent all over me. Good thinking.

I didn't have to ask her if she thought Ginger would care that much. I knew she would. By nature, our vampires were unreasonably possessive.

I thought about what I could say to Ginger if I did decide to tell her about our arrangement. The next text from Tokyo made me think I should wait a while to tell Ginger anything. I wanted to enjoy this.

Does your girlfriend text you during the day?

I thought about it. Did I want to hear from Tokyo throughout the day? We were going to be busy. Today, we were holding a field day for some kids through Types of Hope. The parents could mingle and relax while we tuckered the kids out with games and crafts. I'd be busy and focused. But...

Yes, she does.

Does your girlfriend sext you during the day? That message came with a smirking smiley face. I cringed.

I'm bad at dirty talk. I'm not very creative.

What about tasteful nudes? Like this. A picture popped up, Tokyo in the form she'd taken last night, her robe just open, her nipple just visible. The look on her face was anything but seductive though. She was smiling a big toothy grin. I had to laugh.

I think those will be okay.

Great. You should get going. Chelsea will be around to wake you guys up any minute.

There was a bang on my door. "Up, up, up, Jill. Shower line or breakfast line. Pick one and go!" That's why I set my alarm. Her voice was not the way to wake up. I grabbed my towel and sent a final text.

I'll see you later?

For sure. Have fun!

I wasn't really big on emoticons as a means of communication, but I sent her a smiley face back anyway. And for once, I was actually looking forward to getting back to the house.

❖

Tokyo

Another freaking meeting, but Dalhem called this one so I wasn't too pissed about waiting in Ginger and Camila's place for my sister-queens to show up. The girls were safe out during the day. They knew to look out for each other and, if Ginger insisted, I was sure a few of us would take to wing and head over to the park to keep an eye on things.

I was the first to show up at Ginger and Camila's. Ginger let me in, and I could hear Camila on the phone in their office. Following up with the various fronts that kept the nest running no doubt. Ginger invited me to join her for the final moments of some cooking show, but the peace lasted for a whole six seconds.

"So. What's going on with you and Jill?" she asked.

"What do you mean?"

"Helping her with her homework. And you came out of her room at like what looked like six a.m. We have security cameras like everywhere. You know that right?"

"Hey, I'm just doing what you told me to do. You said be more present and pro-active. Jill is up when I do bed checks. If you want me to ignore her, just say so, but I think you should be the one to tell her why I've suddenly stopped talking to her."

Ginger glared at me for a long moment. I looked back, giving her the Welllll? face. She knew she was caught between a rock and the stupid place she'd created. I was jonesing to call her out on that, but just as I opened my mouth, our Master arrived.

I couldn't hide the joy I felt when I saw Dalhem. It had been weeks since we'd spoken in person, but my reaction would have been the same if I'd seen him hours ago.

"Master," I nearly sighed as I stepped into his arms. He hugged me tight, kissing my hair as we took in the familiarity of each other's scent. Our blood bond was stronger than the ties he held with the others, save Faeth and Kina. He was the original holder of our bloodline. The others were birthed in the lineage of the six other demon-borne from around the world. They followed his rule, and had pledged their loyalty to him, but I was his. He was my reason for being.

He stepped back just enough to see my face. His smile warmed me as he bent to kiss my cheeks. He was in his human form—a tall, gorgeous, dark-skinned Indian man in his late thirties was how most humans saw him. Today his hair was black instead of its normal bright white. He was way underdressed. He usually wore a crisp three-piece suit, but today it was simply slacks and a dress shirt with the sleeves rolled up. And he was barefoot. He glanced down when he caught on to my brief inspection.

"My granddaughter has already destroyed several jackets. Replacing them at this point seems wasteful." He projected the living image of Cleo and Benny's adorable baby daughter J.J. dribbling pureed peaches all over his sleeve into my mind.

"Got it. I'm glad you're here."

"More pleasant circumstances will call for a visit in the near future, I am sure. But I have interrupted something." He turned to the cranky redhead beside me. "My Ginger, you will tell me why you are upset."

"She's mad 'cause one of her feeders likes me more than her."

"That would upset me as well. Greatly."

"That's not it," she said. "It's just…She's just—"

"Ginger," I gasped. "Are you admitting to our Master that you don't trust me? Your own sister-queen?"

The others appeared while Ginger's jaw was flapping in the wind.

"No! That's not what I'm saying at all. It's just, Jill—"

"Ah, my Jill. She is special. You will both be good to her." And that was Dalhem's final word on Jill and whatever was up Ginger's never satisfied ass. He greeted my other sister-queens, including Camila, who had finally gotten off the phone.

"I have met with my children in Texas. Please sit and I will share what is known." We all gathered around Dalhem, posting up on the floor and available pieces of furniture. Then he joined us all across his telepathic link.

Right away, we were in Jessi's memory. It was still daytime and it appeared she was crossing the street on the Texas U campus. Things went black momentarily and then we were in the memory of her vampire, Mary-Anne. I could feel the panic racing in her heart and the pain. Her connection with Jessi was still there, still powerful, but everything about it, the flavor, the feel of it, was off. She flew from campus for miles and miles, at least fifty or sixty miles, from the look of the ground she covered and the changes in the neighborhoods and terrain.

The scene went black again before we saw Mary-Anne in the form of a large dog circling a small rundown house. Another break. They were in an empty room that looked like a shed or a garage. The sun was still up. Jessi seemed calm and normal by all rights, but her eyes were all fucked up, grayish from lash to lash and there was an odd grayish-white spot on her neck. Mary-Anne approached her and then took a step back. Jessi's smell was off.

Not the sulfur and brimstone, but something rotten, like death. Jessi cooed in the dog's direction, but then reached for a large stick and tried to strike Mary-Anne.

Suddenly, Jessi was literally climbing the walls. Mary-Anne was barking at her, charging at her, like she was trying to keep her from going out the door. Then Jessi fell to the floor, her eyes clear. A look of confusion clouded her face, but then the demon presence was back, trying for the door. This went on until sundown, until Mary-Anne's sister-queens and a few brother vampires from their brother fraternity arrived. With a rabbit?

A priest was common practice, but demons were not unique to Catholicism. Evil was universal and everywhere. Mary-Anne turned back to her human form and was able to finally restrain Jessi. The rest played out so quickly. Tarel, a vampire I'd met once, was with them. He performed the ritual to expel the demon, a banishment spell of sorts. The words were in a dead language. I didn't understand them exactly, but with Dalhem's help we had an idea of what he was saying. Tarel was telling the demon to take on another vessel, enticing it to give up control of Jessi. That's what the rabbit was for. As soon as Jessi seemed to come back to herself, she was in Mary-Anne's arms, weeping. Just before the memory cut off, we heard a sickening snap. We all assumed that the rabbit was dead.

Dalhem released us from the link and we did our best to shake off the horrors of what we'd just seen. And felt. I wanted to vomit. Mary-Anne and Jessi had been through so much in just a few hours. They would do what they could for Jessi, but Mary-Anne would live with that pain forever.

"Is that it?" Camila asked. "Jessi doesn't remember who took her or how they got her there?"

"That is all. My Jessi's memory had been tampered with. Nearly wiped."

"So then a vampire helped," Kina said.

"That is not necessarily so. These...creatures share some of our capabilities."

"What do they know about the house?" Kina went on.

"Abandoned many years now."

"Any clue how she was transported there?"

"None."

"What about Jessi?" I asked. "Is she, like, okay?"

"She is fine. I tried to pull traces of this entity's presence from her memory, but her mind could not reconcile the experience of being taken over. I could only hear her terror and her pleas. But her mind has been wiped of the experience, save one small trigger. If she sees her abductors again, she will know."

"Hopefully, they are long gone and too scared to try again." Natasha took the words out of my mouth.

"So what do we do now? Do you think they will try again?" Faeth asked.

"Yes, my angel. I believe they will. This incident appears as if it is a start to something more. My sister-borne has offered to inquire more. Do not worry. We will stop this. And in the meantime I only ask that you watch over our girls. Protect them as best you can."

"We will," Ginger said.

"You will." Dalhem smiled with a calm finality and then he disappeared. The when and how would be up to us.

"Uh, let's just keep doing what we're doing. We'll all stay close to the house. Be more vigilant."

"Should we tell the girls?" Faeth asked.

"Yeah," I said. I completely agreed with her. "How can the girls protect themselves if they have no idea there's a threat?"

"I think we should hold off on telling the girls. I don't think they'll really understand unless we show them Mary-Anne's memories, and I'm not really trying to traumatize them," Ginger said. "They need to be focused on school and their own lives. This is our problem. Let's just keep our eyes open. Okay?"

I didn't like it, but it wasn't like I could disagree. But at least I wasn't on house arrest alone anymore. We'd all be bored out of our minds together.

❖

Jill

My relationship with my pretend girlfriend didn't even make it through the morning. Our community service was fun. The kids were great, and it was nice to meet some of the parents. We got to put some faces to all the bake sale money we raised during the semester, but what got me through the morning was the anticipation of Tokyo's texts. Texts that never came. I thought maybe she was just giving me some time, a little space before she started flooding my phone. Or maybe she was just being considerate of the fact that I was supposed to be playing with a group of young kids.

But I didn't hear from her by the time we got back on the limo buses to take us back to the football stadium. With James and Tim and a few other OBA boys on the team, we always went to their home games as a group. Still nothing from Tokyo as I sat through four quarters of rough play. I figured she'd forgotten about the conversation we'd had that morning. Or maybe she'd just forgotten about me.

The girls talked about the usual things on the way back to the house. Boys, other girls, plans for the night. I'd planned to stay in and watch movies with James and maybe Van over at the OBA house, but then I thought maybe I'd just go to bed. Portia would be out all night, and I'd have the room to myself. It would be a good way to avoid Tokyo too. Even if she were doing her nightly stroll around the house, she wouldn't wake me up. She wasn't like that. When I spoke to her though, when I was ready, I'd tell her I'd changed my mind. A pretend girlfriend wasn't what I wanted either. I wanted something real.

When we got back to the house, there was a party set up for us. A pizza party. Ashley got to the note Ginger left first. "Enjoy. We'll be up at dark."

"We're still going to the Gamma Phi party though, right?" Hollis asked amongst the other girls' muttering. Our sister-queens were always doing things for us, little and extravagant, but this seemed a little random. Our house mother, Florencia, usually had dinner taken care of, delivered, or prepared by the chefs she hired, and we had the option to eat on campus.

And Saturday evening was usually spent getting ready for the night out, but this felt like an event. An out of place event. Most of the girls shrugged it off and either ran upstairs to change or dug into the pizzas stacked on the table. I headed for the pantry.

Our sister-queens' corridors were pretty quiet as I made my way down the winding halls to Ginger and Camila's apartment. It was quiet until I rounded the corner and ran into Tokyo. She saw me right away so it was too late to run or turn and walk the other way.

"Hey. What's wrong?"

"Nothing. I thought we had come to some sort of agreement, but I've reconsidered."

"Jill, I'm sorry. Dalhem came today and we were tied up, but listen, I wanted to come talk to you. Ginger…I…"

"Ginger what?"

"I don't think Ginger wants me around you."

"Did she say that?" I asked.

"No, not in so many words, but I got an interrogation for helping with your project and being in your room last night. I just don't know if this is a good time to—"

"Do you want to be around me?"

"Well, yeah, but—"

I grabbed her hand. "Come with me."

I pulled her farther down the hall until we reached Ginger and Camila's door. You could hear the sounds of sex in the hallway. It was a minute before Ginger answered the door. They did have an hour to kill before sundown, but my God, did they ever take a break?

The door swung open, and Ginger, clutching a robe together over her naked body, pretended to be happy to see me. I was almost too annoyed to ignore the momentary swoon that threatened my heart when I saw her. Her bright hello faded the second she saw who was with me.

"What's going on?" she asked.

"May we come in?"

"Yeah, sure."

I didn't bother sitting down. I just got to the point. "Am I allowed to hang around with Tokyo or not?"

"You are, but I'm just a little confused as to why."

"She's helping me with my human sexuality presentation."

"Again. Why?"

"Why not? You didn't offer to help me."

Ginger might have been undead, but that didn't stop her face from turning neon pink. She cleared her throat. "I'd be glad to help you."

"But you're busy running the house and being with Camila. I understand, but I need an actual reason as to why my being around Tokyo is a problem. I have a partner now, but Brayley is a little too hands-off for my liking and Tokyo is here in the house. And she's awake when I'm awake. Is it just her or is it all the sister-queens you don't want me around?"

"Did you put her up to this?" she asked Tokyo.

"What? No!"

Ginger was doing that thing I hate, treating me like I was a child and incapable of making decisions. I gritted my teeth and did my best not to say something I would regret.

"I think you're not used to your feeders wanting to be around other vampires, but I do. Tokyo has been nice to me when everyone else ignored me, and I'd like to be able to at least talk to her when I want without it causing a huge problem between the two of you. So am I allowed to be around her or not? If not, I'd at least like a reason."

I knew the reason; I just didn't think Ginger would actually say it out loud. Ginger didn't trust Tokyo, or maybe she didn't trust that I was smart enough to handle a vampire who didn't own my blood. But that seemed like a personal problem Ginger had to deal with. Tokyo was incapable of hurting any of us with anything other than an ill-timed overtly sexual comment, and in the short time I'd gotten to know her, I could tell that that version of Tokyo was all a front. I knew what I was doing with the real Tokyo. Ginger was just being paranoid or possessive or jealous. But she had her own relationship, and I was entitled to a personal life of my choosing. It was that simple.

Ginger's eyes narrowed for a moment, and I was positive she'd read my mind.

"It's not entirely…unusual for bound humans to hang out with other vampires. Benny hangs out with Mary and Omi all the time."

"And don't forget Amy and Danni. You hang out with them all the time," Tokyo added.

"Right. Yes. It's very nice of you to help her…Tokyo. With her homework. Thank you."

"Sounds great."

"Yes. Jill, will you give us a moment?"

I hesitated a moment, but then decided they weren't going to talk unless I did. Ginger was going to chew Tokyo out no matter what. Might as well let her get on with it. I headed back up to check out what was left of the pizza, texting James as I walked to the elevator.

Changed my mind. Going out with the girls. You want to come?

His response came before the elevator hit the main floor.

Nah. Game kicked my ass. Gonna stay in. Not with Van or anything.

Maybe going without them was for the best. They could have their time alone, and I could blow off some steam. And then maybe if I asked nicely, Portia would help me get ready for whatever the night had planned for me.

CHAPTER SEVEN

Tokyo

The second Jill was gone, Ginger laid into me. "I don't know what you're playing at, but if you hurt her—"

"You'll kill me. I got it."

"No, you don't understand. I will kill you, and then Camila will kill you, and then I'll have Dalhem resurrect you, and then I'll kill you again. If Jill isn't happy smiles and sunshine every single time she leaves your company, this is all over."

Probably sensing Ginger's unjustified outrage, Camila poked her head out of the bedroom. "Everything okay?"

"Can we not do the tag team hour?" I said with a groan. "You made your point."

Ginger turned around, her voice turning saccharin. "Yeah, babe. Everything's fine. I'll be right there."

I managed not to roll my eyes at the wink Camila threw Ginger's way before she slipped back into the bedroom. Gross. "How about Natasha, Faeth, Kina, and I go out with the girls who want to go out?" I suggested. "And you, Camila, and Omi hold down the fort. That way we have all our bases nice and covered."

"Fine, sounds good."

"Great. I'll see you later. Bye, Camila!"

"Later!"

"I meant what I said."

"I got it."

Done with a pissing contest I hadn't signed up for, I took off to find my sister-queens. I had a little explaining to do if I wanted tonight to go well.

❖

I found Faeth, Natasha, and Kina in Kina's art studio. Faeth was sitting on the worn leather couch in the back corner messing with that damn guitar again. Kina was cleaning her brushes. She'd just finished another piece, a small painting of Benny and Cleo's kid. Probably took her all of fifteen minutes.

She did a double take when she saw me standing there, not saying anything. "Uh, what's up?"

"We're gonna go with the first girls tonight."

Faeth tapped her temple. "Just got the memo from Ging."

"Good. Um, I'm going to stick with Jill for the night."

Kina stopped what she was doing then, and set down the brush she had in her hand. "Is she in some sort of trouble?"

"Yeah, what's going on with the little half pint now? Did Ginger ask you to look after her or something?"

"Not exactly." I explained what Jill had asked me to do.

"So you're pretending to date Jill for her school project?" Kina asked.

"Yes. I was trying to help her figure out what she wanted out of the survey, you know, the ones the girls took the other night, and this is what she said she wanted."

"And Ginger is okay with this?" Kina asked.

"Not exactly. She doesn't know the details, or doesn't suspect them at least, but she did say it was okay for Jill and me to hang out. I just need you guys to kind of pretend I'm not there tonight. For Jill's sake. And my girls. If they think I'm there, they won't leave me alone, and if you guys are hanging around me and Jill, she won't really feel like she's getting to go to a party with her girlfriend, like it won't be a normal thing."

"Uh…it isn't," Faeth said.

"Come on. Are you saying you've never done anything kind of weird for a feeder before?"

"No, I absolutely have, but it was my feeder. Not a girl who belonged to someone else," Kina said.

"Well, like I said, Ginger is okay with us being around each other, and this is what Jill wants. I mean, don't we owe her a bit? We've been black-sheeping the girl for years. She's just lonely. I mean think about it. She asked *me* to be her girlfriend."

"Yeah, all right." Faeth agreed with some lingering hesitation.

"You have a point." And Kina as well.

Natasha came over and touched my cheek. "I think it's very sweet." I knew she would understand. She and Rodrick had stood in as surrogate lovers for me whenever I needed them.

"Thanks, guys. And I'll be there, on watch. Just with Jill. Really, it's the perfect cover." When I explained it that way, the three of them were more agreeable. We went our separate ways then. Kina had two girls coming to feed and Faeth had to check something out for her primary real quick.

Thanks to the sun setting earlier and earlier, I had plenty of time to vanish to the mall. Jill wanted to be with someone her height, but I had no clothes for anyone that short and little. I didn't understand her true struggle until women in two different stores directed me to the kids' section.

When I got back to the house I changed then took a picture of what I was wearing. *How does this look?*

It took a few minutes, but Jill texted back.

Great.

Text me when you're ready to go.

I'm ready. Just waiting for a few people to walk over with.
K. I'll meet you.

I vanished to the front of the house and waited. The fact that I was actually nervous when I saw Jill walking down the front steps with Portia, Navaeh, and Hollis made no sense 'cause I wasn't nervous about Navaeh noticing me or even Faeth and Kina giving me shit for my altered appearance. I was nervous about Jill and whether she would want to see me like this. I was worried I'd embarrass her, say or do something to make her street cred with the girls even less existent.

When she looked at me, her eyes going a little wide and funny with shock, I made myself promise to get this right. I wasn't Tokyo, centuries-old vampire. I was regular Bridgette (no last name, but we'd cross that moat when got to it) twentysomething college junior who thought Jill's overbearing anal attention to everything made her the cutest thing in the world. I had my cover, just had to make sure I didn't blow it.

I waved and smiled, doing that lip bitey thing my girls did when they talked about people they like. Jill waved back. A few more girls came through the door behind them. They were all a-chatter until Jill stopped on the sidewalk in front of me. They all stopped too.

"Hi," I said brightly.

"Uh, hi." She wasn't as confident.

"My car was acting up, but I borrowed my dad's."

"Jaws, who is this?" Hollis asked. I wasn't really impressed with her tone or the way she used the nickname that Jill clearly hated, but I'd rat her out to Camila later. Or maybe I couldn't. I was the secret pretend human girlfriend, not a vampire informant.

Jill introduced me around as Bridgette. "She's in my Arabic class. She's—"

"I'm tagging along to the party with you guys. Thought it would be a good first date if Jill decided to ditch me. Easier to lose me in a crowd." A playful nudge to Jill's hip didn't help her relax.

"A first date?" Portia said. "No wonder you wanted help with your hair. Doesn't it look nice?"

Jill's hair never looked bad. She usually wore her long mass of curls up in a ponytail or a bun, but she'd straightened it and wore it down.

I reached up and lightly touched a strand on her shoulder. "Fuck yeah, it does."

"Can't say shit about her outfit though," Portia added. "I would have helped her out if I knew there was a booty getting situation involved."

"Her clothes look nice too." I laughed, taking in her ABO letterman's sweater and jeans. The other girls were in casual clothes too, all in different combos and swag configurations of red, white, and black. I was glad I hadn't gone beyond a low-cut black shirt and a pair of jeans and sneakers myself. I added a crop hoodie 'cause it looked cute on the mannequin.

"Let's go. I told Marcus I'd meet him down there twenty minutes ago," Portia said, leading the group down the street. I started to hang back a bit after a block or so. Jill got the idea and matched my pace.

"How'm I doing?"

"Good. Do you know any Arabic?"

"Is there going to be a quiz?"

"That's the only class that I don't walk to with James or anyone else."

"Oh. Good thinking. I have some stored up in here," I said, tapping my temple. "I think enough to pass as a level three student. Where is Jim? And the baby Van? I thought they were your roll buddies."

"Oh. Uh, they're staying in and watching movies. I kinda changed up plans on them at the last minute." Then Jill went quiet. We were getting close. You could hear the music thudding in the cooling night air. Fall had finally shown up.

"You okay?" I asked.

"Yeah. I'm just thinking about this on a scientific level. Trying to formulate a clear hypothesis."

"Us?"

"Yes."

"What's the hypothesis?"

"Well, I have no control. We both know we don't have romantic feelings for each other, but we both know that sex is an option, if not the eventual conclusion."

"Go on." I stopped and faced her. This was too heavy for a walk and talk. The fact that she even used the word hypothesis pulled me out of our playful make-believe. I had to see where she was going with this.

"I'm trying to understand the draw to sex, or at least the sudden or gradual appearance of sexual desire. But we did not meet under normal human circumstances. And you're not human and you're coming into this situation with a wealth of knowledge about social and sexual interactions with both men and women. And I know that. So how do I set aside what I know to let things develop organically?"

That was a lot to chew on. Especially when we were supposed to be going to a party. "Hmmm," I said, you know, to keep it light. I started walking again. The girls were getting a little ahead of us, and I needed to keep an eye on them. "If you meet someone on a dating site, you're going into it with preconceived intentions, right?"

"That's right."

"Hold on. Are you more comfortable speaking French?"

"Oh, oui. I mean, goodness, yes! I miss it too. I wish more Americans spoke it."

"Then let's do this in French," I said. In French. Jill's whole face lit up.

"Your French is excellent!"

"Kina and I. She dealt a lot with the French and she encouraged me to learn. Her French is—" Jill laughed as I kissed the tips of my fingers. "But you were saying?"

"Yes. Ah, yes, this feels so much better. Anyway, dating sites."

"Right. Dating sites. Not as organic as bumping into someone on the street or accidentally reaching for the same book in the library. It's not cosmic fate, as you see it, but maybe it is. Maybe it's fate, or whatever you want to call it—destined, meant to be—that you and that person join that dating site exactly when you did and happened to see each other's profiles exactly when you did, and just happened to be feeling brave enough to send the first wink or message, and just the right mood to say yes or wink back. Those stars align right and it just happens that they align through the Internet. Would that make the sex you eventually have any less special?"

"I suppose not, no."

"So how about we look at it that way. I just happened to die and become a vampire and then fast-forward like a shitload of years and you just happen to apply to Maryland U."

"That was not by chance. I picked this school after extensive research."

"Of course you did. Well, what if they'd already accepted a straight-A, biracial, trilingual French-Canadian with gay dads? I mean I'm sure the admissions office has a quota for that. You would have gone to your second choice school, and Dr. Miller's class would have never been on your pre-med track, and you would have never gotten this assignment, and you could kiss the best ABO chapter on earth good-bye. And your precious Ginger." I pinched her cheek then flashed her a big smile. "And you never would have met me. It's kismet, you see?"

"I suppose."

"So if we end up having sex tonight then the stars aligned to make it that way. Or it's because you made a choice. Maybe I stop asking you what you want from this fake girlfriend and keep this form, but I just try to be myself, the side of me that you don't know, but that Ginger doesn't either because she's had her face glued to Camilla's ass since the moment she pledged ABO and she has no clue what any of us are really like. You could get to know me. We could get to a place where you're comfortable, or I do something right that makes you think that being with me wouldn't be so bad. And we totally do it. That's organic."

"Yes." We stopped again. The crowds were in view, the street already teeming with college kids that had probably started pre-gaming hours before. Beer, sweat, body splash. So so much sprayable cologne. A hint of old blood and more than one dog. The OBA boys had brought their Rottweiler, Motherfucker, with them. I could smell him for sure. I focused on Jill and not the music and the noise and whatever Hollis was yelling at some boy across the street.

"But does that screw up your hypothesis?"

"No, just changes it a little, but that's scientific too. Adjusting to new conditions."

"Well, the conditions have changed, my friend. And that said, I'd love to do this." I just kissed her. There was no way I was thinking about it. I just kissed her. It was what I wanted to do. I think kissing her was what she wanted me to do. I thought about that for a full four seconds, and then I realized that Jill was fully engaged in this kiss. She moved a bit closer, tilted her head a bit so our lips slid together in a better fit.

She smelled so nice, like fresh air and cool water. Sweet. And she was soft, smooth. My tongue flicked out for a taste and then I pulled away. My fangs were dropping.

"Are you okay?" she asked.

"Yes." I snarled a bit and forced my teeth back into my gums. The sharp tips were invisible to the humans around us, but they were primed and ready. "Remind me not to bite you."

Jill took a step back. "Can you not control yourself?"

"I can. And I won't." I shook my head. "Sorry. Let me clear something up. I cannot bite you. Even if you want me to, okay?"

The fear that clouded her face told me she knew I wasn't joking. "Why? What happens? Tell me."

"You'll die."

"What?"

"You're bound to Ginger, and whatever this is, the connection has to be broken by Ginger or you before I or any other vampire can bite you. It's stupid and dangerous, but I didn't make the rule."

"Is that why you are so possessive of us?"

"Yes and no. I don't know. We're not human, Jill. Not animals either, but it's primal. You're hers."

"Hmmm."

"Plus you smell good. I'll want to bite you if things go further and you'll want me to 'cause you associate coming with fangs in your neck. But no. No. Bad Jill. No biting."

She giggled at that. "Okay. I won't ask you to bite me, no matter how crazed with arousal I become."

"Excellent. So what do we do now?" I motioned up the street. "A night of reckless drunken irresponsibility lays before you. Your girlfriend, who won't be drinking because she has to get her dad's car home in one piece, is happy to do whatever else you like. Do we go with it, organic like, or do we hit some specific milestones?"

"In my research, it seems that simple touches are the best foreplay. Things like holding hands or touching your partner on their side or back or even anywhere on their thigh can trigger arousal and emotional connections. Consensual touch fosters trust as well."

"You want me to use your body as a Twister mat? Right hand here, right foot there?"

"I actually like to be held. Quite a bit. Ginger doesn't know that."

I stepped forward and put my hands around her waist, then pulled her closer so our bodies pressed together, tits to hip. "Like this?"

"This would work." Her hands found the small of my back through my thin T-shirt. She moved impossibly closer then laid her head on my shoulder. Her body sagging against mine shouldn't have felt as good as it did, and the sigh she let out shouldn't have bothered me as much as it did either.

I stroked her hair for a few seconds more before pulling back, just so I could look at her face. She had the tiniest mole near her eye.

"Wanna go get wasted?" I asked.

"That's organic, right?"

"It is college. Come on." I grabbed her hand and pulled her toward the ruckus.

CHAPTER EIGHT

Jill

Kissing. We were kissing. I was kissing Tokyo. She was kissing me. We'd been kissing all night. In front of people, and I knew the girls would make fun of me, but I didn't care. I never got to kiss anyone like this, not even Ginger when she took our feedings too far and forgot. Forgot something. I don't know.

And then we weren't kissing. All night, stop and start, but I didn't want to stop. I wanted to be kissing. I wanted another beer and I wanted to dance to this song, but kissing. That's what I wanted. Good thing Tokyo was holding on to me. I didn't drink a lot. Or ever. Never really liked it. Not beer at least. I liked wine. Good wine, but sorority girls didn't do wine. They did cheap, cheap beer that went right to my head and made my whole body heavy and my head wobbly. Our vampires could taste alcohol in our blood, and then the girls never invited me out with them. Also, I was underage here in the States. So technically I couldn't drink, but as soon as we got through the velvet ropes—and wasn't that weird?

The Gamma boys worked something out with the school and the other houses in the row and they had the whole block cordoned off with this blue velvet rope. Where did they get that much velvet rope?

"Is there a velvet rope store?" I couldn't exactly see her, but she was with me. Tokyo had a good grip on my hand. I wasn't going anywhere. Even though I knew I could totally float away. I wasn't floating anywhere; her grip was that good. Good grip. "You should be a professional gripper."

Her laugh was like fairies playing with wind chimes. "How many beers is that? Three?"

"I'm French. We know how to drink."

"Are you sure?"

"Oui! Well, half French. That's the white side. The black side is from right here in the USA. Kansas of all places. Isn't that weird? Grandma and Grandpa come to visit us though. They say there's nothing to do in Kansas. I've been there twice and they are correct." I leaned closer because I had to ask her something top secret. "Are fairies real? You can tell me. Or just wood sprites. You can tell me. Really. I can be trusted with sensitive information."

"They might be. I haven't seen one. Are you okay?"

"Mhmm. Just sad."

"Is that why you won't stop dancing?"

"I'm not dancing. My feet are."

"Okay, a little longer then I'm taking you back to the house."

"I'm not a fun drunk, am I?"

"Oh, no no no. You're a perfectly fun drunk. I just don't think Ginger will like it that I stood by and watched you get alcohol poisoning."

"Oh yeah, that would be bad. We can't let that happen. I don't want that. Okay. I'll stop."

Ever so carefully, I made my way over to the curb, and oh so gently set my cup on the curb. It was probably illegal for me to be drinking outside too, but the Greek system at our school always seemed above the law. I'm sure Camila and Ginger were violating all sorts of laws even as we spoke.

That laugh again. Fairies everywhere. "They probably are. You want to sit here for a little while?"

"Where? I'm not sitting. Oh yeah, I am. Yeah, let's sit here." The curb felt good under my butt. "I blew it didn't I?"

"Blew what?"

"My chance to have sex with you? I don't even know where I am. How am I supposed to find your vulva?"

"Going right for my vulva, are you?"

"I don't know. I don't know what I'm doing. What are you doing?"

"Texting Kina."

"Why?"

"'Cause I'm taking you home. Usually, baby, when you hit the point of self-loathing, passing out is not too far away."

"You called me baby. No one's called me that."

"Well, now I have. Up you go."

Tokyo was right. My body had pretty much stopped working. Passing out felt like such a good, good idea. Like sleeping.

❖

Jill

The sandpaper in my throat woke me up. If I didn't drink some water soon I would die. I groaned and tried to roll out of bed. There was water in Portia's mini fridge, but I couldn't seem to get to it. I tried again. Then I scooted a little farther to the end and my feet still didn't hit the floor.

A light flickered on and I thought my head was going to explode.

"Oh, goodness. Turn it off." The light went off again, but I was able to catch a glimpse of Ginger and Tokyo sitting at the end of a massive bed that wasn't mine.

"Here you go." Tokyo put a glass of water in my hand. I managed not to spill it all over myself in the dark and took the most refreshing sip of anything I'd ever tasted in my entire life.

"Thank you."

"Can we try the light again?" Ginger asked.

"Yeah, okay."

I slowly opened my eyes, blinking against the warm glow of the globe light above the bed. I figured we were in Tokyo's bedroom. Everything was black. Everything. Ginger and Camila had a lot of black bedding and such, but they switched things up with reds and golds and greens. I glanced around, and it was black everywhere. Black and hardware. I'd heard that Tokyo was into sadomasochism, but that was something we'd have to discuss at a different time.

"What time is it?" I asked.

Tokyo hesitated a moment before she answered. "It's one p.m."

"No! Oh no. I was supposed to go to the library." I tried to jump up again, but my throbbing head wouldn't let me. I squeezed my eyes shut and lay back against the pillows. Death, take me now.

"Clearly, you needed some sleep," Ginger said with her sweet voice.

"What were you two doing? Were you just sitting here watching me sleep, making sure I didn't aspirate on all the alcohol I consumed last night? And the pizza."

"Ginger wanted to make sure I didn't roofie you," Tokyo said.

"No, I just wanted to make sure you were okay. Tied one on last night, huh?"

"I don't know what that means."

"We learned that Jill should stop after about one beer," Tokyo said.

"I see," Ginger said, trying to pretend that she wasn't fully embracing her protective vampire role.

"I have so much homework to do, but I just want a pile of crepes and then I want to go back to sleep."

"There's leftover pizza upstairs. You want me to grab you some? Or have one of the girls bring some down?" Ginger suggested.

"No. I should go." I glanced up at Tokyo, as best I could. The light was still hurting my eyes. "Thank you for...getting me home last night."

"No problem."

Ginger helped me out of bed, then leaned down and grabbed my shoes off the floor. My phone was banging around inside one of them. "Come on."

She led me out, walking quietly until we got to the elevator.

"I didn't throw up or anything did I?"

"No, you didn't," she said with a little laugh. "We'll move our feeding to Tuesday."

"Oh, I forgot. I'm sorry."

"It's fine. A couple of days won't make a difference. But is everything okay with you?" Ginger asked.

"Yes. Why wouldn't it be?"

"No reason. You just don't seem like yourself lately. You never go to parties and you never drink. Heard some chatter that you were making out with some girl at the party too? Not that you can't make out with people. It just doesn't seem very like you. You usually do Saturdays with Jim and Van."

I shrugged, ignoring the part where she said I was making out with some girl. "Maybe I remembered I was in college. Should probably have some fun before I graduate."

"And that's all?"

"You always tease me because I'm so honest. You say I overdo my honesty."

"You do."

"So trust me. When I say everything is fine, you have to believe that I'm telling you the truth. Or you could read my mind and see that everything's fine." I started running a list of the day's to-dos just in case she took me up on the offer. She suddenly relaxed, so maybe she tried to catch a glimpse. "You should trust Tokyo too. She's a good person."

"I know."

The elevator came and I didn't hesitate to jump on it.

"Drink some more water!" Ginger called out just as the doors slid closed.

"I will!"

The ten-second ride up to the pantry was the last bit of peace I would have for the rest of the afternoon. As soon as I stepped out of the pantry, I ran into Hollis. And Skylar, Kait, Katie, Yazmeen, Carrie, Aleeka. The whole gosh darn sorority might as well have been in the kitchen.

"Ohhhhh, so you did make it back last night?" Hollis laughed.

"Mm, yeah."

"Is your friend okay?" Skylar asked. "It looked like you were trying to eat her face."

"Wait. What! Jill got some last night?" Beth came into the kitchen, yelling loud enough for the OBA boys across the street to hear.

"Did she ever. Here, look at this." I watched as Skylar pulled out her phone. She was enveloped by five other girls. I obviously couldn't see what they were looking at, but I could hear the music from the party and the drone of people's voices. There was Hollis, telling me not to swallow Bridgette whole, and then a second later a bit of a shriek.

Kait looked over her shoulder at me, her eyes wide with shock. "Jill," she mouthed.

"Oh my, God. Will you two get a room!" Skylar said on the video.

My phone vibrated in my shoe and I knew that was my cue to leave. They could enjoy their fun. I needed to shower and eat, assess what homework absolutely had to be done that afternoon, and maybe go back to sleep again. They were still whooping and laughing as I made my way upstairs.

The text was from Papa. It was a picture of a bushel of apples. *Fresh from the market. We're making pies.*

When I got back to my room, I almost texted him back, but I couldn't stop thinking about what had happened the night before. And then I got a text from James.

LOL what the fuck is this and who the fuck is that?

A picture of Tokyo and me kissing popped up. I could only imagine which one of the OBA boys had taken it and sent it to James's phone. I texted him back first.

Long story. Her name is Bridgette. I'll tell you about it later. I'm a little hungover.

Not surprised. Kaleb said you were wasted. Sorry I missed it. LOL

I'm not. Later. Please. I hit send then tossed my phone on my bed beside me.

I'd gotten very drunk. And I'd made out with Tokyo, a lot. I remembered all of that. I didn't remember even seeing Kaleb at the party though, but I did remember what I'm sure the girls were seeing in the video. The moment I'd dry humped her against a tree on the way back to the house. She was trying to get me home. We'd only made it a few feet away from where'd I'd taken a little nap on the curb. It was definitely time for me to get back to the house and in bed, but I was having too much fun drinking, and making out, and trying to get off on my pretend-girlfriend's leg. I was having too much fun with Tokyo.

Thinking of the whole night made me wet. I'd been completely out of control, but I remembered wanting to have sex with her so bad. I remembered how good the kissing was and just how turned on it made me feel. I almost wished I'd asked Skylar to send me the video. Something to remember the night by just in case it didn't happen again, in case our fun was over.

It wasn't about fun though, was it? It was about science. And my theory. I had to see this experimental relationship through until it came to its natural conclusion. That's how real relationships worked, long or short. You gave them a chance and then you could look back and see what you learned, or you could hold grudges while you pretended to move on. So I would see this through, to the sex at least.

I picked up my phone and closed out of James's text screen and went back down to Bridgette's. I typed what came to mind.

Sorry I left in a hurry. I don't think Ginger would have let us talk alone.

The little bubble with the three dots let me know she was already texting me back.

I know. She gave me an earful.

Can we talk today?

Later, okay? I have to be a vampire for a while.

She was making complete sense so I don't know why my heart sank. I'd just seen her. I had just spent the whole night with her. I was pretty sure I could manage a few more hours without seeing her again. I answered her text so she didn't think I was moping.

Yeah. That's fine. I'll see you later.

Yeah, you will. Have this in the meantime.

A photo collage popped up on my phone. Pictures of Tokyo, looking like Bridgette, and me kissing, laughing. Smiling. Cute pictures, nothing like the sloppy display Kaleb had captured. It was something people in relationships did, take pictures of each other, with each other. Smile.

I saved the picture to my phone. Maybe we could take more pictures later.

CHAPTER NINE

Tokyo

When Ginger didn't come back right away, I figured she was waiting for the right moment to properly cuss me out. It made more sense just to go to her. I wanted to spend more time with Jill, as her experimental, fake girlfriend or whatever. Keeping some secrets from Ginger was easy, but I couldn't keep secrets like this. Not from Ginger under her own roof.

I found her back in her apartment watching football with Carrie and Camila. "Come on in," Camila said, nodding toward the open armchair next to their cuddle pile on the couch.

"Thanks. Ginger, can I talk to you for a sec?"

"Yeah, but shhhh until halftime. Like two minutes." Ginger was obsessed with the New England Patriots, but they were watching the Ravens at Arizona.

I sat quietly as the clock wound down to a 14-14 score at halftime. The camera zoomed in on a large black guy as he pulled off his helmet.

"Hmmm, weird."

"What?" Ginger asked.

"LaDanion Warren. I banged him once." Camila didn't say anything, but Ginger flashed me a disgusted look. "What? He feeds Moreland. Camila knows him too."

"I know, but come on. Care, why don't you go grab us something from the kitchen?"

"It's okay," Carrie said. She scooted up to her knees then kissed them both on the cheek. "I have two papers due tomorrow." She grabbed the ABO quilt she'd brought down with her then headed out the door. Once it clicked behind her, I got to the point. The Visa Halftime wouldn't last forever.

"Jill asked me to pretend to be her girlfriend for the sake of her human sexuality project. She has no dating experience. I did not have anything to do with how drunk she got last night, but none of the girls ever want to be social with her, and I think she felt she could unwind because she was with me.

"She wants me to keep this up until she reaches some sort of conclusion to her hypothesis. I just figured since we're all pretending to be some approximation of what we're not, pretending to be her girlfriend for a few weeks isn't that big of a deal."

Ginger's eyes narrowed. "Why you?"

"I told you. Right place, right time. I just happened to catch her when she was up one night working on the shit. I asked her some questions that helped her corral her ideas. I think she appreciated that. And she asked me to keep helping her."

"So you came up with the idea for the survey?"

"I got her there."

"Oh. Well, that makes way more sense."

"Than what?"

"Well. Not to be a dick, but it makes more sense than her actually liking you. I mean—that's not what I mean. It's like you two have literally never talked before last week and then all of a sudden she's asking me if you can help her with her homework."

"I think that's why she asked me. I'm the least connected to her. Maybe 'cause I'm the least connected you," I said since we were both being bitches.

"Okay. Well, as long as it's for science. It's fine."

"I just have one request."

"Please fill me in."

"Don't tell Jill we talked about this. I do think it's important that the girls don't think we're controlling their lives, and this especially? I don't know. She wants this and it'll fuck everything up for her if she knows you're in on the gag so to speak."

"So why tell me? Why not just keep her secret?"

"Uh, 'cause I actually respect you even if you don't respect me. And you'd kill me and 'cause Camila would kill me. But really, even though you've made up your mind about me not giving a shit about anyone, I do. I care about Jill's feelings."

Ginger turned and looked at Camila. Camila shrugged. "I think you know what the call is here, Red."

"Thank you, Camila," I said, a little shocked that she was siding with me. "We used to be friends once, before you got married. I'm glad you remembered that."

She threw me a wink. "I got you."

"Fuck both of you," Ginger whined. "I won't tell her. But I don't know care if it messes with her project, tell me if anything crazy happens. She is mine, ya know."

"Deal. Everything else on the up and up? I haven't heard anything else from Dalhem."

"Yeah, so far it's been quiet. No demon sightings. No feeders have suddenly gone missing. Oh, and Pax was nice enough to cover with the girls last night. You should thank him."

"He's a great guy. I think I will. I'll leave you to your football." I vanished back to my place, knowing that football would only be their focus until they remembered they were attached at the genitals, then they'd spend the rest of the day in bed. I had to make some calls and check in on something for Navaeh, but first I looked up a good florist.

❖

Jill

I didn't see Tokyo at all for the next two days. She sent me silly texts and pictures when she could, but between my classes and the fact that she couldn't set foot outside in human form until after sun down, it made it all that much more difficult to actually keep up with this whole girlfriend thing. However, the more I thought about it, I realized not seeing her would play well into my experiment. I didn't want to date a girl in the house. If Tokyo were a real college student, she'd have her own schedule, her own homework and activities to worry about. I wouldn't be able to see her whenever I wanted. Her absence would add another element to the situation that I hadn't seriously considered. Longing.

Monday afternoon I sent her a text, something to ease the strange pull in my stomach that appeared when I came back to the house to discover she was gone.

Handling something for Dalhem, was the text she sent back.

The pull in my stomach moved to my throat, and I thought for a moment I might be feeling a hint of disappointment. And a hint of jealousy. I wanted to know what she was doing. Ginger and the other sister-queens were pretty transparent with what was happening in and outside of the house, but I knew there were plenty of things they kept from us for our own safety. Given the true nature of what they were, of what Dalhem was, what they kept from us in confidence was definitely for the best. An existential crisis based on knowing that demons were in fact real was not something I needed to deal with just eighteen months away from graduation. So I tried my best to let her absence slide. She had responsibilities and so did I.

Monday night, Faeth did bed check. My smile dropped the moment I realized it was her. She thought I was expecting Ginger though, not her other sister-demon. I didn't correct her when she laughed in a good-natured way.

Tuesday, I was too busy trying to get more surveys filled out to do much texting, and right after dinner, James and Van came to the library with me so I could meet Brayley. She'd gotten a good amount of our surveys filled out, but we only had two hundred, and Maryland University had a student body of about twenty thousand. Dr. Miller agreed to have all of her anthropology classes take the survey, but we still needed a bigger sample.

"Could your sorority set up a table on the quad and just ask people to fill them out as they walk by?" Brayley suggested.

"I suppose I could do that myself. I don't think the girls care about this."

"Well, some of them do. They filled out the surveys pretty seriously."

"No. You're right."

"We can man the table with you," James offered.

"And I'll help you too." I looked up to see Tokyo, or should I say Bridgette, standing next to our table. She was in full college student mode. Messy bun, MU sweatshirt with tattered hood. A backpack that appeared to be weighed down with actual books. "Hey."

"Hey."

"Here. My stats teacher let me poll the class, and I got these from the ladies of Gamma Ro and the Tri Pis." She put another hundred or so surveys on the table.

"Whoa! Thank you." Brayley glanced between Tokyo and me. My face was still frozen. "Um, who are you?"

"Bridgette. Nice to meet you. I'm…um…Jill's. I'm Jill's."

"Oh! That was—" Brayley stopped herself.

"That was what?" I probed.

"Fast. Last week—you know what? Never mind. Thanks, Bridgette. These will help a lot."

"Sorry, this is Brayley and James and Van."

"Nice to meet you," James said, a little smile hitting the corner of his lips. I kicked him under the table. "Ow. What?"

"You know what."

"It's nice to meet you too. Mind if I study with you guys?" She looked at me when she asked the group. Of course I didn't mind, but what the heck was she going to study?

"Ah, sure." I jumped up and pulled a chair over from the empty table behind us. Tokyo sat down and pulled out a copy of Ellison's *Invisible Man*.

"I have to finish it tonight."

"Can we talk for a second?" I asked her. "Come to the bathroom with me."

"Sure."

I excused us and dragged Tokyo to the far stacks, in the general direction of the bathroom.

"Hi," she whispered when we were alone.

"How'd you pull all this together?" I gestured to her outfit, but I was more concerned about the books. And the general impression that she was really enrolled at MU.

"Easy. We have access to the chancellor's office. There's a girl in your Arabic class, Sara something. She doesn't have a single class with anyone else from ABO or OBA. So technically, I *could* be her. I just looked up her syllabuses. Much easier now that everything is online. Omi use to have to hack professors' personal computers, and before that there was a lot of breaking and entering."

"But the homework? You're going to sit here and do homework?"

"What? I like refreshing myself on how creative or wrong humans are sometimes."

"So you're going to sit here and read while we work on our project?"

"Yeah. And I'll help if I can. I thought it would be nice to hang out a bit. I am your pretend girlfriend and all."

"That is true."

"Look, I can leave if you want me to. I get it. Really. This is kinda weird." Tokyo's tone was sincere, like she wanted exactly what I wanted. She wanted what was best for me. I knew if I asked her to go, she wouldn't be offended, and even after that, she would probably be waiting for me at the house and still be my pretend girlfriend. She wouldn't be offended at all. She tilted her head to the side and then reached up and twirled my ponytail.

"No. Stay. You might get bored though."

"Nah. Ellison's a good reread. Let's go back."

"Okay, but I—I wanted to talk to you. About something else."

"Oh yeah, sure. What's up?" She was so much easier to talk to than Ginger. Maybe because my whole being didn't belong to her. Maybe because it was easier to talk to someone when you knew they didn't have you bound to a critical obligation.

"Well, I had a few questions. About Saturday night. And another one about something I saw in your room."

"Yeah, shoot."

"I...sort of mounted you. When I was drunk. I saw the video. I'm sorry."

"There's video?"

"Yeah, Skylar has it."

"Ooooh, I want to see it."

"You're not upset?"

"Uh, no. Why would I be?"

"Because I got drunk and didn't get your consent."

"God, you're great. Okay, listen. One, I can snap you in half, so whether I'm pretending to be human or not, there's no way I wouldn't be able to stop you from doing something to me physically. But I'm glad that consent matters to you. It should. Hold on to that. Two, this kind of clueless, inexperienced thing you have going on, mixed with how eager you get when you just relax has had me like crazy wet for days."

Just hearing her say that turned *me* on. "Really?"

"Uh, yeah. You're a good kisser too. And you were fun drunk. Not wild drunk. I would have told Ginger if you were wild drunk. Or dangerous drunk."

"That's not really me. Either of those…types of drunk."

"What was the other thing you wanted to ask me?"

"I noticed, when we were in your room—" I took a deep breath and just came out with the rest. I had no reason to be shy or embarrassed. "I saw the chains and things in your room. Hanging from the wall."

"Oh yeah, that." She waved her hand between us. "We don't need to worry about that. I used to do that with Cleo. And Natasha and Rodrick. And Camila, now that I'm thinking about it. That's me. Not Bridgette. I have someone for that now."

"I understand that. I am asking because I was curious."

"Huh! Okay. Ginger will try to drain me, but I can show you, I guess."

"Next weekend?"

"But that's Halloween. And you're going out with the girls, right?"

"Yeah…" Halloween was one of the few times during the year I enjoyed doing things as a group. We were all going as food. We picked our costumes out of a hat. I was going as a bunch of grapes.

"I usually have the most fun at my friend Moreland's place. We'll go there some time."

"Okay."

"Let's get back so you guys can science." She took my hand and started leading me back to the table, but I wasn't done yet. She looked back at me when she realized I'd barely moved. "What's up?"

"I want to kiss you," I told her honestly.

"All you had to do was ask."

I braced myself as she backed me against the wall, lightly cupping my face until our lips touched. That was what I had been missing. I'd been pretty drunk, but I remembered the kissing, and I wanted to experience that again, sober.

I knew she was immortal. That was the only way to explain the softness of her lips. And her supernatural existence was the only way to explain how quickly my body reacted to the sweet citrus way she smelled and tasted. I wanted her closer. I wanted her to touch me, all over. Between my legs. It was her magic that made me think I was going to come right then and there.

I kissed her deeply, sweeping my tongue into her mouth over and over. I pulled away though, when I felt her laughing a little against my lips.

"What? What's funny?"

"You. I have to fuck you soon."

"Why do you say that?"

Tokyo gently touched my lower lip with her thumb. "Do you feel how worked up you are?"

"I've never felt this before," I said. I wasn't sure what I meant.

"I know."

"Can we make plans to see each other again?"

"Of course, but normal plans. I don't want to fuck up your experiment. It has to be organic, remember?" She leaned forward and kissed me again. "Tuesday, Thursday, Saturday, we hang out. My dad needs the car Sunday, Monday, Wednesday, see. And Fridays, I have a previous engagement."

"I think that works."

She kissed me again. "Good."

And again.

If I wasn't so eager to tally the surveys she'd brought with her, we might have been at it all night. Or at least until the library closed.

Chapter Ten

Tokyo

Yeah, yeah. I said we should keep things organic. But I had a plan. Another study session at the library Thursday night, with two "spontaneous" make-out sessions in the stacks. Friday night, I'd try to forget she was there during our movie night feeding. That was going to be a little hard, and weird, but we'd get through that, and then Saturday night, late in the Halloween festivities, I'd pull her away and we'd seal the deal.

We walked back to the row, Tuesday night after leaving the library. I'd conveniently parked the decoy car I was borrowing from Omi's wife in front of the OBA house. We said good night to Van and James, and like clockwork, my phone started blowing up. Nine p.m. on the dot, and my girls were checking in. Six texts in rapid succession. Jill followed suit and shot Ginger a text letting her know that she was just outside and would be in in a minute.

I walked her to the door. We said good night. Almost kissed, but Lydia and Ava came sprinting up the stairs and interrupted that. Jill offered to take things back out to the street, back to the car. But I remembered there were things worse than me bumping in the night. I pulled her to the side of the porch. Kissed her in the shadows for a long time, until she was breathless, until I was breathless for air I didn't really need.

Florencia came outside with a cup of tea, to pretend like she wasn't waiting for the rest of the girls to come home. She pretended she didn't see us or know we were there. She watched me skeptically as I said good night to Jill and a shy hello to her. I almost dropped my form when she looked at me, her eyes narrowing further in suspicion. I'm sure that would have affected the pure conditions of Jill's experiment. The fewer people who knew the better. Jill went inside and I drove Mary's Mercedes down to Moreland's where she was letting me stash it. I needed to burn off this energy. I needed to fuck someone and feed. I almost rang Moreland's doorbell. I almost vanished to Juniper's for the blood that would quench a fraction of what was stirring inside me.

But the best thing for me to do was head back to the house. Which I did. I checked on Yaz and Navaeh who were up watching TV. Chelsea, fresh from the shower, was free. I grabbed her for a quick feed and fuck. But that barely worked. I thought about doing rounds after our post sister counseling meeting with D'Monique and Carrie, but the meeting ran forever. When I finally got away, after being debriefed about Ashley and her ED issues and Tierra's parents who were suddenly divorcing, it was almost two in the morning, and for once, Jill was already asleep. I took this as cue enough to get my patience under control. I'd see Jill soon. A hundred and fifty-some-odd years without sleeping with her, almost as long without knowing her. I was fairly certain I could make it a full day and a half without seeing her.

I made it exactly twenty-two hours.

❖

Jill

I was dreaming. James and I were having the weirdest conversation with Papa and the Hulk in a field of black corn.

I kept asking the Hulk where the bathroom was. I had to pee so bad. Finally, I woke up and power-walked to the bathroom. When I came back to my room, my cell phone was vibrating on my nightstand. Had I missed a text earlier? Even the vibrations usually woke me up. It was a text from "Bridgette."

Come outside

I looked at the time stamp. She'd just sent it.

Did you make me pee? I sent back. It seemed awfully weird that she'd texted me the second I'd gotten up to use the bathroom.

What? No. Our senses are freakish. I heard you get up. But you're up. Come outside.

Ginger's not gonna freak out? I sent back. It was two in the morning.

I got this. Just put on something warm and come outside.

I thought about it for more than a moment. It was a school night. I had class first thing in the morning. And what if Ginger wasn't really okay with this? She wouldn't do anything to me, but I didn't want Tokyo to get into trouble. And then part of me realized that I should go. This was what teenagers do, even though I wasn't technically a teenager anymore, but I had missed this part. I'd never snuck out in high school. Never done anything remotely wrong. Never done anything dangerous, if you didn't count offering myself up to Ginger as a dangerous thing to do. I owed myself some reckless fun.

Okay. I'm coming.

I gathered up my things, including my keys, my phone, and my student ID badge, out of habit, and went to the bathroom to get changed. Portia wasn't a light sleeper, but if she woke up, I'd rather be gone than have to explain to my roommate why I was hopping into my jeans in the middle of the night. The rumors of my new girlfriend had already made their way around the house, but I didn't want to add to the gossip train. Once I was ready, I crept down to the study lounge and hid my pajamas under the couch. No one would check there before I got back.

I'd had the quiet of the house to myself plenty of times, but I never knew how quiet it was when I was distracted by my homework. I tiptoed down the stairs in the near dark. Just the two dim sconces on the stairs. The alarm on the front door was usually armed at 9:30 p.m., but I saw the little flashing green light at the port above the door. Tokyo must have deactivated it. I stepped outside, closing the door behind me, but I didn't see Tokyo anywhere. I jumped when I heard the alarm beeping, like it was suddenly armed.

And I jumped again when Tokyo appeared suddenly in front of me.

"Goodness!" I gasped. "Don't do that."

She laughed because giving a twenty-year-old a heart attack was hilarious. "Sorry. You ready?" she asked me in French. It was easier to respond in kind.

"Sure. Ehr...where are we going?"

"Don't make me ruin the surprise. Come on. Let's go." I let her take my hand, and we started walking. Down the stairs and on toward campus.

We walked in silence for a long time. The Row was surprisingly quiet. The OBA kept the same curfew as we did, and most of the other frats and sororities also had some sort of check-in time, but I knew the OBA boys had their late foolishness from time to time. I expected to at least hear a little commotion as we made our way through the private township, but I barely heard a peep. That quiet scared me. The farther away we got from the house the quieter it seemed to get. I could only hear our steps and our breathing. I wanted to say something, but the idea of creating a noise scared me even more.

Tokyo squeezed my hand and pulled me a little closer.

"Tell me about Jill," she said finally, as we crossed the first major street. That put us on the main campus. Still, no one was around that I could see.

I swallowed, scanning the trees and buildings in front of us. "You already know everything about me. You know everything about all us girls."

"I know what we have on file so to speak." She tapped her temple. "And all the tidbits we've gleaned from being around you over the years, but I want to hear you tell it."

"There's nothing to tell. You know I have no life. I have two friends and you know them. All I do is study and organize chapter wellness events. I want to be an OB/GYN, and I don't want to open my own practice. I want to work in a clinic, and you know that's why I've wanted to learn more languages. I don't really have any hobbies. I'm an okay dancer. That's me."

"You used to bake too. Why don't you do that anymore?"

That hit some sour notes. I felt my throat close up a little. I missed Dad and Papa.

We were at campus center now, just near the library. There was a man asleep on one of the benches outside. My nerves shook again when I saw him move. What was it about being out on a night like this that scared me so much? We both kept quiet until we passed him.

Tokyo bumped my shoulder. I still hadn't answered her question. "Tell me."

"My dad is a pastry chef, but you know that too. That's why he came to Montreal in the first place, but I'm sure you knew that too."

"I didn't, actually," she said. "I mean we get the goods on your parents, but unless you're a legacy or there's some huge red flag, we don't get all the dirt."

I didn't know if she was telling the truth, but that made sense. What would she need to know all about my fathers for? "Oh.

Well, he and Papa…that was our thing. We created, we brûléed, we powdered, filled, glazed…we baked. Like all the time."

"And you used to bake all the time when you first moved into the house. What changed?"

"Benny graduated." It was weird to say it out loud. I didn't have those feelings for her anymore. And I had figured out that they were based more on physical attraction and infatuation than real feelings, but there was something about Benny. She tolerated me and I think she made the others girl tolerate me too, as much as they could. But after Benny left…I looked over to see Tokyo peering at me as we walked. Really looking at me. "You weren't expecting me to say that."

"You really loved her, huh?"

I shook my head. "No. I just had a crush on her. And her breasts."

"Benny does have huge tits."

I don't know why that made me laugh, but it did. "It's strange that you remembered that about me. That I liked to bake so much."

"Steel trap. Fun part of being undead. Brain like I don't know what. We keep everything upstairs."

"I know. I just never thought you noticed."

Tokyo gasped, like she was offended. "What do you mean? You brought all of us sister-queens cookies and cupcakes all the time. There were those mixed berry tarts and then your cake pop phase. That shit was good."

"I just—I thought you didn't eat it. Ginger didn't eat everything I made her."

"'Cause her mouth was filled with Camila cunt. Kina and I would sit up in her studio and pig out, all the time. But you were just baking for Benny that whole time?"

"Hmm, it's weird that you think that I loved her. Not weird. But accurate. It was about love. That's what baking was about for me. I wanted Benny to love me and I wanted the other girls to like me. Plus we have bake sales eighteen times a semester so it's not like my skills went completely to waste."

"But when Benny left?"

"I think she took whatever tolerance the girls had for me with her. And then I think Skylar and Hollis were nice to me to get me out of Cleo's way when they got back together. Once Cleo was gone and they were bound to Ginger, it was like they didn't care anymore."

"They still call you Jaws."

"Yup. Last year, on the first day, I heard Hollis telling the new girls that I was the most annoying girl in the house and that they could feel free to tell me to shut up any time. So I just stopped talking around them unless I have to. You know, chapter business and stuff. "

"Jill."

"I know."

"Does *Ginger* know that?"

"No, and I'm not going to tell her and neither are you. That just makes me a tattletale, and the girls already don't like me. It would solve nothing. Anyway, it's not like I joined the sorority to make friends. It'll look great on med school applications."

"I'm sure it will. You should bake again. Not for the girls, but because you want to."

She still didn't get it. I wanted to explain to her that I never baked for myself, and neither had Dad or Papa. We baked for others, for each other. For people we loved, and since no one in my life fit that mold—

"Or you can just bake for me," she said as she came to a sudden stop. We'd made it to the other side of the main campus. She was smiling at me when I faced her, practically showing all her teeth. Her fangs were hidden though.

"How do you hide your fangs like that?"

She winked at me. "Magic."

"No, really. How do you do any of this?"

"I'll show you later. Let's go inside, shall we?"

I looked up at the letters above us, coming out from the marble in gold relief. Evans Recreational Center. I did not work out, and I'd only been over to Evans a few times, two of those being the campus tours I took when I first visited the school and on my first day as a freshman. "What are we doing here?"

"Still not telling. Still a surprise." We walked up to the front entrance, massive royal blue double doors with large brass handles, a little black box with a blinking red light just above. The spot for me to swipe my ID, if the place was open, and if I wanted the university to have a record that I'd been there.

Tokyo turned to me. "Don't move, okay? For real. Stay right here."

"Okay."

She vanished again, but what felt like not even a full two seconds later, one of the doors creaked open. She waved me inside. "Come on."

Inside, the Evans Center was even scarier than outside. The long hallways stretched out in front of us. The only light came from the decorative security lights in the courtyard garden that framed the track, but the light just made the corners and shadows creepier. I grabbed Tokyo's arm as we passed the front check-in desk.

"You want me to turn on the lights?" she said before she leaned over and kissed my head.

"No," I whispered, my voice quaking. "I'm fine."

"I'll protect you. Don't worry."

She took me through the halls down to the ladies' locker room. The automatic lights in there flicked on, and I might have screamed. Tokyo definitely laughed at me. "Shut up!"

She led me through the short maze of lockers and showers right out on to the pool deck. The pool itself was massive, but it was overshadowed by the three-story-high windows that ran the length of the building. More light poured in from outside, and with the flick of some invisible switch, the pool glowed a pretty shade of aqua blue. The deck was hot and muggy, and before we made it to the middle of the large pavilion, I was already sweating. I thought about shedding my coat, but I still had no idea what Tokyo had in mind.

"We're going swimming?"

"Something like that." Tokyo took a few steps back and then a few more. And then she started getting undressed. I watched as her clothes started to pile up on the bench beside her, until she was completely naked. "You coming?" she asked, but before I could answer, she dove into the pool.

I watched her body weaving through the water, under the waves she created. Just watched until my brain reminded me that I could get in the pool too. I didn't have to watch. I could participate. I toed out of my boots and practically threw my clothes on the bleachers. I dove into the pool, thankful I could swim. When I surfaced, Tokyo swam toward me and backed me against the white tiles of the shallow end.

"Hold on to me. I've got you—"

"What?" But she'd already gone back underwater. She was between my legs, pulling my thighs over her shoulders, lifting me up and out of the water. My nipples hardened immediately in the cooler air. I thought to cover them, but my hands automatically went to the top of her head. Her mouth was on me. My yelp of shock turned into a cry of, "My goodness!"

Her tongue.

Her fingers.

She was stroking me, rubbing her fingers up and down. I couldn't feel the wetness of her tongue, but I could feel the pressure of it, each sweeping stroke and the sucking of her lips as she took up an alternating rhythm. Lips, then tongue, lips and then tongue. I should have told her beforehand. All of that wouldn't be necessary. It wouldn't take that much.

I came, hard. My vision going out for just a second as my cries echoed off the walls. But she didn't stop. Tokyo kept on licking and sucking until I actually pulled her hair. I pulled hard, so hard I was worried that I'd hurt her, but it was the first thing I thought of, after kicking her in the back with my heel. She gave my ass a final squeeze, my lips a final kiss, and then she slowly lowered me back into the water.

She came up, blowing a bit of water out of her mouth as she smiled. "We've got to get you a safe word. I like having my hair pulled too much."

"A what?" I panted.

"Nothing. Did you want me to stop?"

"Yeah. Yeah, just for a sec. I don't know if it's the feedings or what, but I come so fast. I mean, if I'm the slightest bit turned on all you have to do is touch me a little and it's over."

"But you were turned on?"

"We're naked. You're naked."

She pinned me against the tiles again. She kissed me. "All this chlorine and I could still tell how good you taste. Do you want to taste me?"

"Yes."

"You okay?" she asked in that tone again, the sincere one that told me I could tell her anything and it would be okay.

"Yes, I told you. I'm not very good at dirty talk."

"I'm okay with that." Tokyo swam around me over to the ladder. When I realized what she was doing, I followed. The shallow end was...shallow, but that didn't mean a whole lot when the very top of your head didn't clear five feet. I wanted to go down on Tokyo, but not while I was trying to tread water. She must have figured this out because she swam over to the ladder and sat up on the top rung. I followed, stepping up between her legs, standing on the bottom. The rails on the ladder didn't give her much room to spread her legs, but she must have figured that out too because she scooted forward a little. So she could show me everything.

This isn't her body, a little voice said in the back of my head. *But it is and you want her. You don't care.*

Her...everything was perfect. The color and shape of her thighs, her labia that had just a little bit of closely trimmed hair. Was that even her natural state, or if she went back to her normal form would it go away? And her breasts were perfect. Big, but not too big for her body. Light brown tips. A small waist, but not tiny. I looked at her belly button for a really long time. Bridgette would have it pierced I think. That's what Bridgette would do. Or maybe she wouldn't.

I must have blinked or maybe I started crying. I couldn't tell with all the water dripping out of my hair and running down my face, but my throat felt like I was crying. So did my chest. I plunged myself back under the water.

When I came back up, Tokyo was off the ladder. I was in her arms. I didn't know what was wrong with me. She was right. I'd never done this before, not without the help of Ginger's bite and what it did to me. I had no idea what I was doing, touching another girl's body, and I was terrified that I was going to fuck it up. I just didn't expect the panic to come so fast or to be so overwhelming.

"How about we stop pretending?" she whispered against my ear. "You really be yourself with me. Really let it out. Forget about Ginger. Forget about the girls. It's just you and me. I might be slightly important, but base brass tacks, I'm still human and you can be as human as you need to be with me."

I swallowed and tried to scrub my eyes. "I want to talk dirty with you. I actually thought I could try something sadomasochistic with you, but I just looked at you, this naked body, and I freaked out. You were right. I've never had sex before. I slept with James once, but that didn't count, and it doesn't count if it doesn't count, right?"

"Right. It only counts if you say it counts."

"Well then, I've never had sex before. The stuff with the feedings doesn't count. That's like a chapter meeting, but we're all naked. But it's a part of the job. I want to help Ginger, and I love the feedings, and sometimes I like fooling around with the girls, but it's not organic, it's not real. This is."

"It is. I like you, Jill. I wouldn't have gone through all this trouble breaking and entering if I didn't."

"Okay, well, I want to keep doing this, but I have to be honest with you. In my mind, the way I feel right now, I might as well be a virgin, and I'm terrified I don't know what to do. Also, I'm kind of afraid of the dark. Did you ever notice the night light in my room?"

"I did. And that's okay. Scary things happen in the dark. How about this? We stop acting like we're in a porno. If I remember things correctly from my first time seven hundred years ago, it didn't start with in-pool oral."

"What did it start with?"

"This." She kissed me again. I kissed her back, but it took a moment for me to shake the emotional tremors that made me feel absolutely inferior to whatever she was offering. Her willingness to participate in this thing I had to label an experiment for it to make sense to me.

We kissed some more, and I felt her lifting me. I didn't want to know where we were going; I didn't want to watch the weird shadows dancing around the pool. When I did open my eyes, we were in the light and the warmth. We were in the sauna in the women's locker room. We kept kissing as Tokyo laid me down on the warm, towel-covered benches. I didn't have to imagine how she found time to set it all up.

"Are you okay with this?"

"Yes."

"How about this?"

She climbed on top of me and slipped her hand between our bodies, but instead of touching me, she touched herself. I glanced down and watched. I became a little transfixed with the way her hand was moving, the sounds she was making. The back of her hand brushed against me lightly. And then again and again with a little more pressure each time. My hips were rising to meet her cupped fingers. I moaned too.

CHAPTER ELEVEN

Jill

We made it back to the dorm just before sunrise. Portia was still asleep when I climbed into bed. We'd rinsed off after our time in the sauna, but my hair still smelled like chlorine. The smell of it made me smile as I fell back to sleep again.

But I wasn't smiling when I woke up ninety minutes later to the sound of my alarm. Late was one thing for me, but all night? That was not my territory. It was a struggle to get in the shower. Almost impossible to do my hair. I gave up short of not even moisturizing it, but I knew the cool October air would leave it a dry, brittle mess if I didn't at least throw some leave-in in it before I put it up.

Walking down the stairs, I had no idea how I was going to make it through three ninety-minute lectures without falling asleep. I'd needed coffee, even though I never drank it. Or some sort of energy drink. I went into the kitchen where breakfast was laid out for us girls. Florencia was there, enjoying a massive cup of coffee herself and reading something on her tablet.

"Good morning," I said, greeting her with a kiss on the cheek.

"Mhmm. And these are for you," she said. I didn't even notice the bouquet of flowers on the counter beside her. Orange, yellow, and pink peonies I think. The note was handwritten, not printed. My name was on the outside, and on the inside it said, *I hope this counts, love B aka T.*

I pulled out my phone and sent her a text.

It definitely counts. Thank you for the flowers and thank you for last night.

We had sex in the sauna for at least an hour before we went back out to the pool to splash and play around. We ended up making out again and then having sex again. I was so nervous, but Tokyo made it easy. I knew how to deal with these things in groups or through the erotic haze of feedings, but I had no idea what to do one-on-one. Luckily, Tokyo knew how to defuse my embarrassingly timed panic attack. She made me feel comfortable and safe and not at all like a bumbling novice.

"You still want coffee?" Florencia asked. She was standing there, pot in hand.

"I—no."

"They're very beautiful," she said, nodding toward the flowers. Did she know who really sent them?

"Thank you. I'm just gonna go put these in my room." Of course the handful of girls I ran into had something to say. The bouquet looked perfect on my desk. I hid the note, though. I didn't know the bounds of Portia's nosiness.

When I got outside, James was waiting for me to walk to class. Autumn and winter were starting their not-so-delicate dance. I shoved my hands in my pockets, wishing I'd grabbed my mittens.

"What's up?" I asked when I saw the look on his face. Something was up and I had a feeling what that something was. I'd shut down all his attempts to talk about Bridgette, but eventually I was going to have to explain.

"Not much. So Bridgette. She seems nice."

"Thanks. She is. She's very nice."

"And cute. You can tell she likes you a lot too. Why didn't you mention her before? I thought we were supposed to be best friends, Jilly Bean."

"I still hate that name."

"I know. But what gives? You never even mentioned meeting her and then you were all over her at the Gamma party and then she's showing up to study. She's coming tonight too, right?"

"Probably."

"It's not like I mind. I mean, yeah, I mind. You tell me everything and I tell you everything. And you just take everything so seriously and you plan everything down to the letter and then boom, girlfriend out of the blue. And she's not even an ABO girl, which might have made a little more sense."

"No, it wouldn't. They all hate me and you know that."

"It's because they don't know you."

"Don't do that, okay? You and Van choose to separate yourself from the guys. You choose to spend less time with your brother, but when it's time to do stuff together, Tim and the boys don't give you shit. They don't make you feel unwanted. Tim even told me he wished you hung around more."

"I know. He said that I'd replaced him with you as my twin."

I almost told him the truth right then. I was creating unnecessary tension in our friendship, but I didn't know what he would say. Or maybe I did. James always made me laugh. Even when I was stressing myself out or taking things in a way he thought was too seriously, he was always my voice of levity. And that's what made it hard for me to tell him. He would crack jokes, and if Tokyo came around in her Bridgette form, I knew he would tease her or try to get her to do something to drop her human façade.

And I also thought he might laugh at me. I was one cash transaction from having actually hired a girlfriend, and even though I knew it was all a scam, something temporary that wouldn't last, I was starting to feel things for her. Or at least starting to grow attached to the way she was making me feel. How did I explain that without sounding like a completely naïve idiot? I couldn't.

"I didn't want to say anything until I knew how she felt about me. I've done one-sided before."

"Hey, we've all had our hearts broken before."

I wasn't going to bug him about Van, but I glared at him. "Okay, well, we've thought about having our hearts broken. I get why you did it. Rejection can be embarrassing."

I glared at him again.

"Okay, fuck you," he said, laughing.

"You know I will never, ever give you a hard time about any of this. I just want you to be happy."

"I know. I just need two good seasons in the pros and then I can come out. Making myself invaluable is key."

"I know. I still think you should tell Van how you really feel about him. It's obvious it's way more than sex with you two. It's not like he would out you, and you wouldn't out him. You two can be there for each other until you're ready. You already are."

"I know. We fucked again last night and then he stayed in my room. Tim hung with the guys down the hall so we could have the room to ourselves."

"See! And you're worried about me not telling you anything."

"Well, Bridgette seems cool. I'm gonna put her in a headlock if she hurts you." There was that humor. I had to laugh.

"Please don't. She's not ready to take on one half of the Tongan powerhouse."

"Damn straight she isn't."

"Let's stop at the Eagle's Nest. I need a few energy drinks."

"Late night?"

"I snuck out with Bridgette and we broke into the pool over at Evans." I felt a rush of adrenaline just sharing a bit of my adventure.

"What! Oooooh, Babineux. I'm telling your sister-queen."
Something told me she already knew.

❖

Tokyo

The next few days were interesting. And good and a little weird. I had to split my time with the girls and handling my responsibilities with Dalhem. He asked Kina and me to do a little asking around, talk to bound vampires, see if they'd heard or seen anything unusual, but it was business as usual across all the land. The rest of the time, it became apparent that I was dating Jill. She took a couple of afternoon naps down in my place. That was the good part. The weird part came Friday night.

Our feeding movie night went off as planned. And as always, I gathered my girls to our corner of choice. Chelsea wasn't feeling too well. An emotional snafu with her boyfriend, but she wanted to at least feed me before she went up to her room, to sulk or make up with him. She was gone before the title sequence for *Pacific Rim* even popped up on the screen. And so was Jill. I don't know why I expected her to stay.

I had to keep shit nice and normal, and nice and normal meant partaking in a minor orgy with my feeders.

It's not like I expected Jill to sit on the other side of the room to watch, and I didn't expect her to come over and try to join us, but I wanted her to stay. I wanted her to try to join us. I wanted her to be with me. I saw the night through, feeding from and fucking the girls until all three of them gave up. D'Monique and Yaz wanted to stay in my bed, but I was able to convince them to take their after-party up to their room.

It was nearly one a.m. when I got back to my place and got in the shower. Faeth and Omi were on house duty til sunrise.

Natasha had gone across the street to hop on her husband's dick 'cause six sorority girls weren't enough to wear her out. They weren't enough for me either. I wasn't on house arrest anymore, and there was always Moreland's. She was always happy to see me. And so were the strippers at Tens. I'm sure Kina would have been down for an x-rated field trip, but none of that was working for me. I checked my phone. And then checked it again.

I texted Jill.

Hey, are you still up?

Yeah. Watching TV on my tablet.

Do you want to come down?

Yes.

K. Door's open.

It only took her ten minutes to show up at my door, but those ten minutes made me realize just how much we took our ability to jump through space for granted. Stairs and elevators and doorways were for chumps. It gave me time to put on a shirt though. Jill was getting used to me, but I wasn't sure if she was up for full frontal nudity. Though I'm pretty sure that might make at least some of my intentions clear as fuck. Some shorts and a shirt did the trick.

When she finally arrived, I was more than ready for her. The feeding and fucking frenzy had only made me more horny, and I hadn't done anything but kiss her since our time in the pool. And that time in the pool. God, Jill was shy, and yeah, she freaked out a bit, but once we found her comfort zone? Fuck. Being with her was like a dream. Eager defined everything about her once we got into that sauna. If there wasn't the small issue of the rising sun I would have kept her there well into the morning.

I opened the door for my sweet little thing before she could even knock. Maybe eager was my problem tonight. I looked down at her in her pajamas, ABO sweats and an ABO tank top. She had her tablet tucked against her chest. She looked cute but sleepy, like she'd really been dozing off when she got my text.

"You tired?" I asked, tucking a few loose curls away from her eyes.

"No. It's just been a long week."

"Well, come on. Bed or couch?"

"Bed."

I nodded and let her lead the way. I'd made sure to turn all the lights in my place on. The all-black decor made it feel like a dark cave. I liked it like that, perfect for doing dirty dark things, but I wanted my guest to be comfortable.

I sat on the bed as she looked around.

"What were you watching?" I asked.

She looked at her tablet. "Oh, it's called *South End Girls*. British show—"

"Oh yeah, it's a comedy. About the four girls in high school? Faeth loves that show."

"You've seen it?"

"Yeah, a few episodes. We can keep watching if you want."

"No. I—I'm still pretty wound up from feeding Ginger. Sometimes I do something about it, but—"

"That's what I'm here for. Is that what you're saying? Oh, do you want me to change forms?" I was still in all my five nine glory.

"No, it's fine. I think the height difference bothers me the most if we're out walking around or if I'm out in a crowd. I hate having to look up all the time, but I like you like this too. I like the real you."

"And we don't have to stand up."

"That's true."

"Did tonight bother you? I mean me and it seemed like you left faster than usual."

"No." She shook her head. "I've never really cared for them, the group feedings. Although I suppose I don't really *want* to watch you with the other girls."

"I know. I guess it isn't permanent. I—"

"You what?"

"I don't have to stay here forever."

"How long *have* you been in the house?"

"About seventeen years?"

"How long do you have to stay?"

"Our Master asks for four years minimum, but most of us stay longer or leave and come back. We like hanging out with you guys."

"How long will you stay?"

"I don't know. Things are different now."

"How?"

"Meh, let's talk about that another time. What do you want to do tonight?"

Jill pulled in a deep breath then squared her shoulders. "I think you know by now that I like to…research. I was thinking about the other night in the pool and your taste for sadism."

"Did taking you to the pool seem sadistic?" Wow. Had I fucked up that bad?

"No, no. I meant, when you were in control I felt much better. I felt comfortable. I think my…little breakdown had as much to do with inexperience as possibly not wanting to take the lead. It's like how bad I am with dirty talk. I like when you talk that way, or when you ask me questions. I like that, but I'm so bad at reciprocating."

I grabbed her shirt and tugged her between my legs. She caught on enough to ditch her tablet on the bed.

"Are you saying that you want me to dominate you?"

"If that's okay with you. I think I remember you playing the submissive role when you were with Cleo." I almost laughed. She sounded like an adorable BDSM textbook. I reached for the ties on her sweatpants and started to undo them.

"I can switch easily. Well, I think we'll skip the sensory deprivation stuff. No blindfolds, possibly gags later, after we've had some practice."

I pulled her sweats down and her underwear with them. I could smell how wet she was, the sweet musk that was wholly unique to Jill Babineux and Jill only. She watched me as I slipped my hand between her legs, pulled up her tank top so it wouldn't get in the way. Fuck, she was so wet. I looked up at her as I slid my fingers back and forth along her clit. I don't know if I expected her to look away, but she didn't. She met my gaze with a steady, almost neutral expression. If it weren't for the subtle movement of her throat and the way her pussy seemed to grow even wetter, I would have thought I was doing something wrong. I spread my fingers apart, spreading her open.

"Do you want me to tie you up?"

A little nod. "Yes."

"On the bed or standing up like this?"

"I want to stand up."

"Good. I like you this way. Don't move."

I vanished from my spot on the bed over to my chest where I kept most of my toys. I hadn't used them in ages, but I still had a pair of soft leather cuffs. The real metal handcuffs seemed a little too extreme. Plus, as much as I wanted to, I didn't want to leave any marks.

I appeared again behind her. I loved that little gasp of surprise.

"Give me your hands."

She turned around and presented me with her wrists. That wasn't what I meant at all, but it didn't matter. I'd make her come with her hands behind her back or not. I secured her wrists in the cuffs, then turned her back around as I circled to sit on the bed.

"Hold your hands up, like this." I guided her hands up so her fingers were just touching her left shoulder. Her forearms completely covered her tits right along with that tank top, but that wouldn't be a problem for me either. "Don't move until I tell you to."

"Okay." There was a slight tremble in her voice, but I could see it in her eyes, in her stoic expression, she was ready.

I moved quickly, but not fast enough to hurt her, and yanked her forward, pulling her body against mine. That tank top was easily bunched up and shoved up under her wrists, leaving the underside of her breasts exposed. Jill's tits were perfect. Small, with dark brown nipples that were just barely peeking out. I ignored them though, and just laved at her belly with my tongue. I nipped at her with my teeth, with my fangs, but I was careful, so careful, not to draw blood. I felt the tremors run through her body when the sharp tips scraped at her skin. God, I wanted to take her so badly. I knew her blood had to be downright delightful, but I would get even the smallest of tastes over Ginger's dead body and over mine. And if I fucked up real bad, over Jill's dead body.

I nudged her arms a little higher, laughing to myself at the little noise she made, part discomfort, part discovery. I found one of those tiny nipples and sucked it into my mouth. That almost made her crumble. She sagged against me, almost all her weight leaning on my side and shoulder, but I didn't care. She was just making it easier for me to reach what I wanted. Making it easier for me to reach around and wet my fingers on her sweet pussy from behind. I closed my arms around her, forcing her legs to squeeze tighter on my hand, forcing her slippery slit to pinch and squeeze on itself, giving me more of what I wanted.

My hand was soaked and so was she, so it was nothing for me to play with her ass, just to tease her a bit.

There was that look again, almost too serious, too calm, but she was down for it. Her teeth pulling on the inside of her lip.

"You tell me no," I said. She had to know she was in charge. She was the one in control of what happened next.

"I'm not telling you no. Not yet."

I pressed just the tip of my finger against her puckered hole. Not even in, just against, rubbing and pressing, spreading her juices around. I knew as well as anyone how good a nice deep anal pounding felt, but I also knew how the lightest touch in just the right place would make me purr like the creature I was.

"You're growling," Jill said quietly, her voice hiccupping at the end.

I let go of her nipple long enough to answer. "Do you know what that means?"

"That you're turned on?"

I moved my hand, rubbing my index and ring finger along her dripping folds while I continued to play with her ass with my middle finger. "It means I want you so bad I could eat you."

My fangs dropped all the way and I had to grind my teeth, practically crack my jaw to get them to recede.

"You can't bite me," she said. She was close.

"I know, babe. And I won't, but I want you to come."

"Don't you have to make me?"

"I suppose I do."

I slid my other hand between us, shoved two fingers into her warm cunt. That was all it took. She was coming all over my hands. Her orgasm radiated through me, like it did with all my girls. I felt her pleasure in the tips of my nipples and between my legs as my own come soaked the fabric of my shorts. It was the natural, normal, magical sort of thing that always happened when a human that belonged to me experienced pleasure or pain. I felt it to my core. It shook me so deep that I had to ignore the why and focus on Jill and the real limits of her pleasure. It was the only thing I could do to keep from going crazy and sinking my teeth into her throbbing vein.

CHAPTER TWELVE

Jill

I was out of my depth for sure, but nothing Tokyo and I did in her room before I finally had to sleep seemed the least bit sadomasochistic to me. And neither did the things we did when I woke up again...or before I had to get ready for community service. I looked up all of the sex acts we participated in, and none of it seemed the slightest bit kinky.

Maybe I just didn't understand the word, or maybe we needed to do something more extreme, like put me in an electrified cage while forcing me to perform oral sex. I don't know. Maybe the cuffs made it something more. They did add an element that could be labeled bondage. When we got back from the Types of Hope center (today we just assisted with a mass mailing and handed over some more funds we'd raised), I tried to write down my thoughts about our night together while Portia was in the shower.

Interested in bondage.

Am comfortable letting T control the situation. Could also be construed as being a submissive.

I also added *Enjoy kissing* for good measure.

We did much more than kiss, obviously. As she'd already shown me that night in the pool, Tokyo was very creative. When I thought I was out of orgasms and energy, she would find some way to make me come again and again. It was hard for me to come out and say just how badly I wanted to reciprocate, but I think she understood that that was exactly what I wanted. I guess that's also where the submission came into play, but I didn't really see it as submitting at all. She told me she was going to sit on my face. I was okay with that of course, and just used my mouth to pleasure her. She took my hand and used it to get herself off. Again, I was completely fine with that. I enjoyed it.

When I got the chance, I would ask her to explain submission and sadism more thoroughly, because I was still really confused. Maybe I could put that on my survey.

I don't understand sadomasochism, and I wanted an expert to come to Maryland University and give a seminar on the pros and cons and why anyone might find an interest in it.

Portia came back in the room and started to get ready. We were heading out to the Kappas' Halloween party a few houses down. She was going as a bunch of grapes too, but I knew she'd find a way to make things more glamorous. I was going with something more cutesy.

"How was your night?"she asked. Out of nowhere. Which was really strange because other than passing on basic sorority related information, we never really spoke to each other.

"Sneak out with your girlfriend?"

"No.

"Oh. I saw you leaving Tokyo's room this morning. I figured maybe she helped you get out of the house. If anyone would help us break Ginger's rules, it's her."

"Yeah. She was helping me with my presentation."

"Are you sure about that?"

"Yes, why wouldn't I be? Why are asking me questions? What do you care?"

"Jesus. Calm down. I just figured Tokyo was giving you relationship advice."

"Oh. Why would you think that?"

"You're missing or with her all the time and then suddenly you have this hot girlfriend. I figured she was giving you tips on how to communicate with other human beings."

"Are you trying to be nice, because that wasn't very nice."

"Anyway, I was just going to say if you want pointers from like a human and someone who was born this century, you can ask me."

"Did Ginger ask you to say that?"

"No." She looked at me like that was the most random thing she'd ever heard so I decided to take her word for it. "I think I figured Benny rejecting you had broken your will to date and fuck or something, but clearly, I was wrong. And then I thought maybe you just hated us, and then I realized you'd have pretty good reason to. We are kinda mean."

"I appreciate that. I think."

"I heard that Bridgette girl is pretty nice so that's cool. Is she coming out tonight?"

"Yeah, I think so."

"Cool. You need help with that let me know." She nodded to the grape costume I was trying to lay out on the bed. "We should have gone with something better. Six of us are going as bananas."

"Next year we should be more proactive when it comes to selecting these things."

Portia laughed. "Seriously. I bet the Rho Gammas are gonna show up all cute and we're gonna be a big doofy buffet mobbing the place."

"You're right." I realized I was laughing too. With Portia. That was an absolute first. The only thing that made sense next was to run for the shower.

❖

I came down the stairs feeling like a complete moron. I saw Carrie at the bottom of the staircase in her green grape costume and realized she looked stupid too. I thought of wearing cute pigtails, but the grape leaves of the costume were attached to this purple skull cap that covered my shoulders, neck, and practically my whole head. Portia was nice enough to help me shove all my curls back into the thing, but the final result left a lot to be desired.

"Oh, thank God," she called up at me "We both look terrible. Come on. We're taking pictures."

All of our sister-queens were there taking pictures on their cell phones like proud parents on prom night. There were little groups of food all over the first floor posing and preening.

"Where's Tokyo?" I heard D'Monique ask.

"She had plans," Ginger said. "But she told me to take pics of you guys. Don't worry. She'll see how cute you all look. Jill, come on in the front. Carrie, you too."

I came around front, trying to ignore the way my stomach was jumping. Was I Tokyo's other plans, or had she bailed on me too? How would her feeders feel if they knew she'd intentionally ditched them to be my date for the night? They wouldn't find out, I tried telling myself, so why would it matter?

We took a million more pictures. Then finally, finally, I got a text.

I'm outside.

"I'm gonna start walking over," I said.

"Wait, we're coming," Chelsea said. She and seven other girls were slices of pizza.

"Jill's just anxious to see her girl, aren't you?"

"Hey!" Ginger yelled before the first of us could get out the door. That got our attention, along with Faeth's ear-shattering wolf whistle. "Stick together please. I know you all look out for each other, but Halloween nights are always filled with extra weirdness—"

"And people being dicks," Kina added.

"That too. So please, heads on a swivel. And if anyone is too drunk to make it home, please call us. We'll come get you."

"Yes, Ginger," we all said in unison.

She snarled at us playfully, but she knew it was her own fault, our loving dictator.

I tried not to push my way through the throng of food Tierra and Taylor were leading toward the front door, but knowing Tokyo was waiting for me outside made it hard not to shove Taylor out of the way. The twenty seconds of patience paid off. Tokyo was waiting for me on the brick path outside our house. Tokyo posing as Bridgette. Dressed like a can of soda.

"See? Now we can be grape soda," she said in French the moment I walked up to her. My only thought was to kiss her, so I did.

The Kappa party was a mess. Too many people, not enough alcohol to even remotely go around, and then the brothers of Psi Omega decided to show up as a whole NBA basketball team, complete with black face. A moment after I saw them walk in the door, I got this overwhelming feeling that we had to leave. I grabbed Tokyo's hand and started heading for the door. When we got outside, I realized all of the girls and our brothers from Omega Beta Alpha were leaving too.

"Did you do this? Convince us to get out of there?"

"It wasn't just me. Kina was in there too, and so were Omi and Faeth." I looked behind us. I didn't see them. What form were they taking? Were they dressed up too? Do you guys do that a lot, influence our decisions?"

"No, actually. We'd love to, but it's rare for us to be in the right place at the right time to sense this kind of thing."

I tried to search my memory for times I'd suddenly changed course and avoided a bad situation, but only one came to mind. The night a huge brawl broke out before the homecoming football game my sophomore year. Our whole chapter had left the bonfire minutes before the fight spilled into the crowd and dozens of people were injured. I knew mind control was something our vampires were capable of, and though the idea of being controlled never sat well with me, I was glad they'd gotten us out of there. We weren't even a block away and we could hear a commotion inside.

Portia had tips on two other parties, but those both turned out to be a bust. A handful of the girls and a few of our frat brothers broke off to see what was happening down at the LGBTQ Center on campus. Finally, Josh, the OBA president, invited us back to their house. He assured us with a text from Rodrick that there would be booze, games, and music. I knew I'd have fun, especially with James and Van there, especially now that James was cool with the idea of Bridgette, but I had high hopes for my first Halloween with a girlfriend, even if our relationship wasn't exactly the real thing.

We'd almost made it back to the OBA house, but I stopped short of the elaborate brick path that lead up to their front door.

"What's up?"

"I want to do something else. We can hang out at the OBA house anytime. It's Halloween. Let's do something."

"You're just taking advantage of the fact that you know I can come up with something, something good," she said, glaring at me.

"Well, yeah."

The glare morphed into a mischievous smile. "Okay. Text James and Portia and tell them we're going back to my house in Ellicott to watch movies. I'll let the others know you're with me."

"Okay. Where we going?" I was a little over-excited, but I was starting to like Tokyo's brand of adventuring, even if it did include the dark.

She leaned closer, as close as she could with our costumes in the way. "It's a surprise."

❖

The surprise involved a drive down to the waterfront. I was a little nervous when she turned down a long, long alley between the storage warehouses. I'd never been down to this part of the waterfront, and from what I understood from the Internet and the news, this was where you came to get murdered or at least be a victim of some type of crime.

Ahead, one of the large doors swung open and light poured out into the alley. We pulled into a very plush garage and parked next to two brand new Mini Coopers and an Escalade.

The garage door closed behind us and another door inside sprang open. A curvaceous white girl with blond hair skipped toward the car. She was dressed up like a puppy. In a way. She had her face painted up like a dog, and she had on fake floppy brown ears, a black studded dog collar, and a brown tail, but other than that, she was naked. The only other things "covering" her were the black paw print pasties over her nipples and between her legs.

When Tokyo stepped out of the car, she was Tokyo again. The soda can costume still fit, but of course, she looked different. The girl ran over and hugged her as I stepped out.

"We didn't think you'd come!" the girl said.

"I wanted to show Jill some things."

"Oh my God. You guys are grape soda! That's so fucking cute. Are you sure you want to change?"

"Uh, for what I have planned, yeah," Tokyo said. "Jill, this is Krystal. Krystal, Jill."

Krystal waved and bounced on her heels instead of shaking my hand. "She's one of Ginger's?"

"Yeah, so—"

Krystal made the gesture of locking her lips and tossing the key. "Not a peep. I swear. Come on. I got the stuff you need. You can change in my room."

"Ready?" Tokyo asked me.

"Um, sure." For what?

Krystal turned and led us into the warehouse. And when she turned, I saw that her tail was actually a butt plug, lodged securely up her ass. I had to wonder how bouncing around with that thing felt.

Krystal's room was interesting. It was very bright and colorful, but it also looked like a room set up for, well, a dog. There was a food bowl and a water dish in the corner. Her bed had a canopy draped over it in the fashion of a pink and white doghouse and the front had "KRYSTAL" on it in rhinestones. She had a regular vanity; there were paw prints all around the mirror, and next to that was a rack of various collars and leashes. Plush toys and novelty dog bones were strewn all over the place, the floor, the bed, every corner.

Once she left us to change, Tokyo started to get undressed, but I was still in awe of my surroundings.

"Krystal's a submissive that's into puppy play, or pet play."

"So she pretends to be a dog, or a puppy?"

"It's hard to explain without proper context. You'll see in a sec. Let's get ready. We're missing the real party."

We both changed out of our costumes, and Tokyo threw me the outfit I assumed she'd picked out for me during a conversation I had no clue took place. She handed me a short black skirt, a black bra with black ruffled bloomers, and a fishnet shirt. She completed the look with a pair of platform Mary Janes that actually put me over five feet. It was a great costume for me because I would never in a million years pick out this outfit for myself. I sat still while Tokyo did me up with a ton of black eye shadow and fixed my hair into the pigtails I'd wanted to wear in the first place. She finished off the look by placing thin but soft leather cuffs on my wrists and a leather collar around my neck. She managed to tuck my ruby necklace safely under the leather.

"It's just for decoration," she said with a wink. Tokyo slipped on a fishnet sheath dress, with nothing on underneath. She put on some stilettos with metal heels that made her another foot taller than me. Once her hair and makeup were done, she walked over to where I was waiting on Krystal's bed. She cocked her head to the side as she looked me over.

"Leash or no leash?" She meant for me to choose even though I thought she was the one in charge.

"Uh, I think we can do the leash. That way you won't lose me in the crowd."

"Good thinking." Tokyo plucked a black leash off Krystal's wall of accessories.

"She won't mind?"

"Nah. Krystal and I are buds. And she picked out your outfit."

"Oh." I held still as she hooked the leash to the ring on the collar.

"Perfect. Let's go have some fun."

Clearly, the exterior of Krystal's home was misleading and every room in the interior was soundproof. We doubled back down the hallway toward the garage, but made a left instead of a right. We passed several closed doors and then Tokyo opened a huge metal door that opened onto a big open room that was filled with people engaged in various…activities.

I have to say, being a member of ABO prepared for me some of what I saw. There was a Halloween party going on. Music playing, decorations hung from the ceiling. Costumes altered in interesting ways to allow access to different body parts. There were a few people in furry costumes—two foxes and a white cat. The most eye-catching thing I saw was going on, literally, in the middle of the floor.

A naked woman who looked a lot like Sophia Fillamorrow, Baltimore's current mayor, was kneeling beside two young guys who were splayed out on their backs. They both had fake pig noses and ears on, and pink leather strapped around their chests and hips. That was all they were wearing. The woman who really looked an awful lot like the mayor, had their penises between her hands, and she was rubbing them together. They were both laughing and moaning. A few people yelled for them to squeal, which they both tried to do before breaking into fits of more laughter.

On a nearby couch, a man dressed as a commercial airline pilot, who I quickly realized was a vampire, was getting a blowjob from an older man dressed as a female flight attendant. They had my attention for only a few seconds though. The squealing on the floor brought me back to center stage. Tokyo seemed fine with letting me watch. She just stood there beside me, not saying anything. Maybe she was letting me absorb the shock.

"You are most certainly hell-bent on having me drawn and quartered." I looked up as a very slim, very tall woman in a pornified Marie Antoinette costume came sidling up to us in her gold heels. Thick white powder covered her face, but I saw her fangs when she smiled. She bent and kissed Tokyo on the mouth. Then she looked down at me. "Welcome to my home, Jill. I'm Moreland. Can my Krystal get you anything? A snack? A beverage? A mostly naked boy?" Her Southern accent was so thick.

I was thirsty, but I didn't want to send Krystal to wait on me. Also, I was a little afraid to speak.

"I think she'd love some water," Tokyo said with a little squeeze to my hand. "It's been a weird night already."

"Water coming right up." I watched as Krystal hopped off her spot on the floor, where she'd been watching the action. She disappeared into the crowd.

Tokyo and Moreland continued to talk, but I was watching the floor. One of the boys arched his back sharply off the floor. I thought he was going to come, but he seemed to be fighting that urge. His body sagged again and he regained a bit of his composure. It looked like the other boy was about to come, but it looked like he was pinching his own leg to stop that from happening.

"It's a game we play sometimes." Krystal seemed to appear next to me with a red cup full of water. "Whoever comes first gets a punishment and the winner gets a prize."

I took a long sip. I had to thank Tokyo. I was dying of thirst. "What's the prize?" I asked.

"You'll see. Tokyo, can Jill come watch with me?"

"Why don't we both join you?"

"Yes, yes. Please. I'll be right with you," Moreland said.

We followed Krystal and found a good spot on the floor, right near the woman and the two boys. Tokyo sat first then gestured for me to come sit between her legs. She wrapped her arms around my waist as Krystal plopped down beside us. The woman we were watching was definitely the mayor.

"Give in, Luke!" Krystal yelled at one of the guys.

"No," the taller one with brown hair groaned. "And fuck you."

A bunch of people laughed, including Tokyo, but I was still too caught up in what was going on to come up with any sort of reaction.

"You okay?" Tokyo whispered in my ear.

"Yes." But I couldn't help but shiver when she kissed my neck.

"You wanted to know more."

"You're right. I did."

"Are you wet right now?" she asked bluntly. Her lips and tongue were still teasing my skin. Just then, the boy who wasn't Luke came all over the mayor's hand, Luke's penis, and his own stomach.

"I am now," I said bluntly.

Tokyo's breath rushed out against my skin as she laughed. Her hand slipped between my legs, and she cupped me roughly. I squeezed my eyes shut. I loved her gentle touch, but this felt so much better. The coarse fabric pressing against my clit was exactly what I wanted.

The chaos went on in front of us. The boy who lost, Davey, apparently from the taunts and instructions he was following, crawled to his knees and cleaned off Mayor Fillamorrow's hand and Luke's penis and hips with his tongue. When he was done, the mayor shoved a pig tail plug into his ass.

The whole time, Tokyo was rubbing and grabbing me. I knew there was a chance that she would make me a part of the spectacle, though I saw that I already was. Another couple, two women who both appeared to be human, had started fooling around on another couch. One of them was watching us. She seemed to be grinding to the same rhythm as Tokyo's hand between my legs.

"You can come when I say so. Do you understand that?" Tokyo said in my ear.

"Yes, but why?"

"Because I'm not ready for you to come yet. That's how this works, you submitting to me. Do you understand?"

Luke stood up and finally claimed his prize. Mayor Fillamorrow's mouth. She gripped his hips and took his painfully red erection into her mouth. Davey handed her the other pigtail plug and that went right up Luke's ass.

She started sucking him off. Krystal called out first, but soon half the room was chanting, "Come! Come! Come!"

A smile flashed across Luke's face, but it was gone just as quickly, replaced with a look of pure determination. He gently grabbed the back of the mayor's head and started thrusting his hips. I could tell the mayor was smiling around his penis. She was having a great time. I was really close to coming.

"And if I don't want to submit to you?" I shuffled, trying to shift her hand closer to my hole. The fabric of the bloomers was still in the way, but that didn't matter. I wanted the pressure.

"Then I stop and we just enjoy the party. What do you want?"

"I want to submit."

"Good."

Tokyo's hand stopped moving.

Luke came in the mayor's mouth as the crowd around us cheered him on. Tokyo's other hand slid up my neck, and she tipped my head back. Her tongue was in my mouth, moving around, searching, exploring, making me wish she'd keep touching my clit. Making me wish her fingers were inside me making me come.

When she let me come up for air, she started stroking me again, reminding me that an orgasm was nowhere in my near future. I wondered what my prize would be if I could last, what my punishment would be if I just gave in to the urge to come in my borrowed bloomers right then and there.

I watched the mayor stand up and kiss Luke on mouth. Cum dribbled down both their chins.

CHAPTER THIRTEEN

Tokyo

I got Jill back to the house way before sunrise. The girls usually rolled in between one and two on Saturday nights, so I figured if we split by one, I could squeeze her back into her grapes and back to the house before Ginger had reason to scream at me for keeping Jill out all night. We did cut it close though. I'd planned to try to make her go a few days without coming. She'd been desperate for it throughout the night, and I thought it might be fun to tease her for a few days until I surprise fucked her in the stacks at the library during one of her study sessions with Brayley. But I couldn't make it back to the car.

I thought it would make sense for Jill to shower in Krystal's room, wash off the crazy amount of eye shadow I'd smeared on her. Somewhere between taking off the collar and the wrist cuffs, something in my blood told me it was time to fuck. I pulled her on top of me on the bed and had her ride my fingers until she came all over my hand and lap. Again, I came when she came and decided to ignore that frightening fact, again. And then I followed her into the shower and had her eat my pussy. Watching the water wash the dark makeup off her face was such a turn on, I came on her tongue, then pulled her off the floor so I could taste myself on her lips.

The look on her face when I pulled away, the look that told me she was more than okay with this shower being the start of our night, was the punch in the face reminder I needed. It was time to get home.

Somehow, I knew Ginger was going to find out that I'd taken her to Moreland's, but I had two things working in my defense. One, Moreland barely talked to Jill 'cause she was too busy hosting and fucking. Two, Jill had a great time. When I wasn't teasing her, she and Krystal were talking or teasing Luke. They danced a little, took some selfies, and Krystal herself explained her deal with the puppy play. I wasn't one hundred percent sure Jill got it, but on the way home she told me that living full-time with Moreland and not having to work probably relieved a lot of stress for Krystal, and allowed her to tap into and indulge more dedicated fantasies. I wanted to tell her that Krystal had been into puppy play before Moreland scooped her up, but I didn't.

Jill had a way of thinking about things. She was literal like me, but her chain of logic was different. I saw Krystal's submission as a part of who she was, and so did Jill, but she tackled her comprehension of the whole situation from a practical standpoint.

In her mind, Krystal was a full-time submissive who was comfortable expressing her interest in pet play because she was free of responsibilities. And then it occurred to me that maybe Jill was living her life that way, defining her every move, expressing her every desire (or not) based on what she thought she *had* to do. Jill had spent her two years of college practically avoiding the kind of fun she wanted to have. And I had to wonder what she was and was not doing with her life due to her own sense of responsibility. I had to wonder what the girls in the house and how they withheld their friendships and kindness was doing to Jill. Why was she double majoring? Why hadn't she tried dating outside of the house before?

Did she even give a shit about this elaborate sex ed project or was it just another responsibility to fill her time, to fill some void?

I felt like I knew the answer to all of those questions, but there was only so much I could do. I couldn't derail her academic plans, and I still couldn't order the girls to be nice to her, but I could be nice to her. I could keep spending time with her the way she wanted me to. The way I wanted to.

I think I was falling for Jill.

I didn't hear a peep from Ginger until that night. Around eight, she was in my head with a *911-get-over-here-right-now* message that was mostly yelling. Five seconds later, she sent a text. When I saw that it had gone out to the group, I knew something was up. When I showed up at their apartment and our brother-kings from across the street were there too, I knew something was really up. I hugged Rodrick and Pax before Ginger told me to sit down.

"I'm sorry to meet with you all like this, but it's urgent. I've just heard from Francois down with the Beta chapter at Carolina, and one of their boys has been killed. One of Rudy's. A junior named Javier."

The shock in the room was palpable. We all knew we could lose a feeder at any moment. We did what we could to hold off disease, but accidents happened, crimes were committed. If Ginger and Cleo weren't undead proof of that. But the pain was still overwhelming. Losing a feeder, losing a feeder young, was the worst feeling in the world.

"We think the same thing or something like what went after Jessi, went after him as well," Ginger said.

"What do we know for sure?" I asked.

"We have this video." Our brother-king Franklin turned around the laptop he was holding. He'd cued up a security video. A young guy ran down a brick path to the street just as a blue, late model SUV pulled up. "This was right outside the house. And those are his parents in the van. Ten minutes later, he tweeted, 'Parents surprised me with a visit. Ditching my two o'clock for some Waffle House.'"

"Twenty minutes after that, Rudy said he started feeling Javier's distress," Rodrick said. "But he could not pinpoint the cause of it, the nature of the feeling. He said it felt chaotic, exact, and muted all at once." Which was strange. We felt our feeders' every emotion, but to keep from going completely insane, we learned how to sort those emotions and sensations into categories of urgency. A paper cut didn't even catch my radar. One being murdered on the other hand…

"Approximately an hour after things started to feel shaky, Rudy lost him," Rodrick said. The thought of it was like a killer punch to the gut.

"Where did they find him?" Omi asked.

"About fifty miles from Durham. Small, rundown town in the middle of nowhere. In an abandoned house, same as Jessi. Marks all over his body, but it was his own skin and blood under his fingernails, like he'd been trying to claw himself out of his own body," Franklin said. "Francois had the presence of mind enough to at least photograph the scene and his body."

"When we caught up to his parents, they were already back home with no recollection of ever leaving town to surprise Javier," Pax explained. "Dalhem's with them right now, trying to re-create their mental day."

He'd wipe their memories immediately after. Clear every trace of himself and give them the memory of a new day. A day when they didn't accidentally lure their son to his death.

The usual routine would kick in after that, everything that typically happened when one of our humans died of a mysterious cause. An alternate crime scene would be staged, if it was needed. Fires worked well a lot of the time. Then one of our people with the local police would be contacted. They'd handle the paperwork and reach out to the parents. The family would take it from there, and us immortals and the few humans that knew the truth would mourn. Wonder why with all our powers, the sheer strength of our blood and the magic it allows us, we couldn't be there to protect them. I felt terrible for Rudy.

"We stay pretty focused on our collegiate nests. Has there been any word of any feeder outside of our network being kidnapped or attacked?" Kina asked.

"We have to tell the girls," I said. Kina's question was valid, but protecting the girls under our roof was all I could think of.

"I don't know—" Ginger started.

"Look, I know we don't want to scare them or give them overwhelming information that they just don't need to know, but if something is out there targeting them, they *need* to know. How can they protect themselves, how can they look out for each other if they have no clue what they are looking out for?"

"I have to agree with my sister, Tokyo," Franklin said as he nodded to Rodrick. "I want to tell my boys."

"It'll give us more protection and time to get a read on what the fuck this thing is and what it wants," Faeth added.

There was a bit of silent communication between Ginger and Rodrick. I'm sure Camila was involved too because she was always invited to the party. Finally, Ginger caved.

"Ugh, I hate this. We're supposed to protect them. I feel like it's going to cause a panic."

"Hey, that's the point of us talking now," Natasha said. "So we can come up with a plan to avoid a panic."

"I know. Kina and Pax, contact all the collegiate nests and let them know," Ginger said. "I'll speak to Dalhem about telling every vampire. I know he's had his eye on the whole region, but so far it looked like whatever it is just started targeting our feeders."

Rodrick walked over to Ginger, taking her by the shoulders. "We will protect them. We'll find a way."

Ginger smiled weakly and squeezed his hand. Then Rodrick and our other brothers vanished.

Ginger turned to Camila. "Let's text the girls. Emergency chapter meeting at nine fifteen."

We all took that as our cue to hit our assigned task. I wanted to reach out to our feeders with the Feds right away, see if any suspicious deaths or missing persons cases had popped up in our area. But Ginger had other ideas.

"You. Stay."

I eased back into my chair, ignoring the looks Faeth and Omi gave me before they vanished. Yeah, yeah. I was in trouble with the moms again. What was new? I kept my mouth shut, though, and waited for Ginger's groundless yet inevitable temper tantrum.

"I'd think very carefully before you answer."

"Okay. I'm still waiting on the question."

"Where did you take Jill last night?"

I looked at Ginger and Camila by default because they were practically sitting on top of each other. What the hell was Ginger playing at? Did she not feel Jill walking down the hall right that second? Or had she planned this so she could interrogate us both?

I watched the corners of her eyes shift when the knock came at the door and then her nostrils flared. What the fuck was going on?

"Come on in, Jill!"

Jill opened the door then stopped when she saw me. "I…I just got the text about the emergency meeting, but it's my turn to feed you. I thought I'd come down first. What's going on?"

"We're just talking about what we did last night," I said, trying to keep my voice calm. This was not a good place for me to be, between feeder and demon, but it was too late.

Jill, on the other hand, seemed to have no problem with our current situation. "You heard how the Kappa party went. I asked Tokyo to take me somewhere else. We went to a party at a friend of hers, Moreland."

I squeezed my eyes shut as the name left her mouth. Camila actually started to growl.

"And I don't understand why that's a problem," Jill went on. "Moreland was very kind to me, and I really like her feeders. They were nice to me too."

"Did Moreland try anything with you?" Camila asked.

"No!" Jill and I said at the same time.

"Okay, what's the deal with this Moreland woman, and why do you and Ginger insist on hating her so much?"

"Moreland was raised well before reconstruction, and I think she's held on to a lot of beliefs around slavery. She thinks that our feeders are tools for her pleasure, and I—"

"Oh my God! That is not fucking true!" I turned to Jill. "Like a million years ago, Camila and Moreland had a really awkward sexual encounter, and Camila never forgave her for it, and then somehow their minor differences in opinion regarding sex and feeders blew up into this huge convoluted thing. Ginger doesn't even know Moreland beyond like two conversations, and her hatred is one hundred percent based on how Camila feels about her."

"Did she try to force herself on you?" Jill asked Camila. Her voice was shaking, which really pissed me off because she had every right to be concerned if that was actually the case. Which it wasn't.

Camila took her sweet ass time answering, but at least she told the truth. "No. She didn't. I simply don't—"

"You just don't like her," Jill said. "Yeah, I know how that goes. We had fun last night, and Moreland's feeders are happy. Very happy. She's good to them."

"And she's good to me. She's been good to us, or are we forgetting how she came through when Cleo died? I would never associate with someone who tried to hurt one of my sisters. Never." And Camila knew that. I wasn't so sure about Ginger. I ignored the knot in my throat and focused on my hand. What had happened to us?

"I thought you said you were going to trust me and Tokyo?" Jill said to Ginger.

"I do."

"No, you don't. I got home last night before half of the girls. I didn't drink. I didn't do drugs. Tokyo was by my side the whole night. I asked her to take me somewhere off campus, but somehow she's in trouble. But for what?"

"Why are you two together?" Ginger asked, but the truth had already dawned on Camila.

"'Cause they're sleeping together."

"What? But you told me the relationship was pretend, for her project," Ginger blabbed.

"You told her that?" I couldn't stand the hurt in Jill's voice.

"So she wouldn't question who the fuck this Bridgette person was and why she was suddenly around and why she had history."

"So you two are sleeping together?" Ginger asked.

"Yes," Jill replied.

"I'm only going to say this once."

"Somehow I doubt that," I muttered.

"You shut up. Jill, I think about who you are and what you want for your future and who she is and her past and her future, and I think this is a bad idea, okay? This might seem like fun now, but I know you, Jill, and I know you've been hurt and I know how big your heart is. No matter how you slice it this shit show spells disaster for me."

"How are you this much of a hypocrite?" Jill said so matter-of-factly I actually snorted. "You were younger than me when you turned and married Camila. You knew her just as much, actually less than I know Tokyo now. Amy told me, it was like what, three months? I've been around Tokyo for almost two years now.

"Yeah, she's sarcastic and doesn't always do things exactly the way you want her to, but her girls love her, and even during all that mess with Cleo and Benny she was still nice to me. She has *always* been nice to me. So yes, we are sleeping together and kind of dating, I think. I'm not sure, and maybe that will end and I'll be heartbroken or maybe she will, but it's not fair for you two of all people to say that we can't just because you think you're trying to protect me."

"Did Amy tell you I was never human? Did Amy tell you that I hadn't even finished puberty when I was changed, but that I was born with so much vampire blood in my system that I had dormant powers, that there was a possibility I was already immortal?"

"Well, no. But—"

"That's the difference between you and me. You have your whole, short human life before you and I want you to live it."

Jill squared her shoulders and pulled in a deep breath. "So do I, and during that life I want to say that I had a relationship with a vampire named Tokyo and that relationship played out naturally with no interference from the vampire that I feed."

Ginger looked at Jill for a long time. I wanted to scoop her up and kiss the shit out of her. Finally, Ginger looked at Camila, the other half of her brain, where sense lived. Camila kissed Ginger on her forehead, and what was done was done.

"Fine. Jill, please stay. I do need to feed. You can go," Ginger said to me. "But you still have to be there for your girls. Jill doesn't take precedence over them."

"That's how it's been. I haven't been neglecting them at all."

"And you're okay with that, Jill?"

"Again, almost three years. I'm not blind or naive."

"Fine."

I stood and almost kissed Jill, but I thought better of it.

"And, Tokyo?" Ginger said just before I vanished.

"Yeah?"

"Maybe when you get a chance you can tell Jill your real name."

I wanted to jump over the table and claw her eyes out, but I settled for a smile and a nod. I walked over to Jill and was glad when she let me kiss her soundly on the lips. And then I vanished. I could hit up our government contacts in D.C. before I had to get back to meet with the girls.

CHAPTER FOURTEEN

Jill

I was really angry with Ginger. I couldn't understand why she thought Tokyo and I were so stupid. Of course I didn't think Tokyo was her real name, but that was the name she liked to be called, so that's what I called her. And yes, I understood that Camila wasn't exactly comfortable with the way Moreland lived her life.

But at the end of the day, the time I spent with Tokyo had nothing to do with Moreland, and as long as Tokyo and I held up our ends of our respective blood pacts with the respective parties under the ABO roof, Ginger had no right to be so cruel about us being together.

I had not expected to develop feelings for Tokyo during our little experiment, but now the feelings were there. Was it forever love? Probably not, but that wasn't always the point. She would be my first girlfriend, not my last, and that was okay. I wanted to enjoy the time we had together, without Ginger's and Camila's supremely biased opinions getting in the way.

I did feed her though, accepted several orgasms as payment, which also worked against Ginger's master to plan to ensure my loneliness because the whole time she was at my neck I was thinking of Tokyo and how badly I wanted to be with her.

We wrapped things up just in time for our emergency meeting. I was so angry, I didn't think to ask Ginger or Camila what the meeting was about while we were still in private. I left them to have their own conversation and headed for the TV room. On my way, Tokyo sent me a text.

Are you okay?

I texted her back right away. *Yeah, I'm okay. Ginger didn't suck me dry for my insolence.*

Lol, that's not what I meant, but I'm glad you're not dead.

I'm sorry about what she said.

Can we talk later tonight?

Yes, I was hoping we would.

Find you later.

She added a few heart emoticons. I fought the urge to text back exactly what I was feeling and settled for a few emoticons of my own.

❖

Most of the girls were already in the TV room when I got upstairs. I took up a post by the window next to Portia.

"You want me to send you these?" She held out her phone and showed me a picture of a bunch of us dressed as food products from the night before. "Swipe left."

I did and there were two pictures of me and Tokyo. Grape soda. We were kissing.

"Bridgette's cute," Portia said.

"Yes, I think so too. Please send these to me." I handed her phone back, and a moment later, it vibrated in my lap.

"No problem."

My phone vibrated again and once more just as our sister-queens arrived. I tried not to focus too much on Tokyo. She joined her girls in the corner, leaning one arm on D'Monique's shoulder.

I couldn't say or do what I wanted, now that she was in the same room, but I could send her something. I texted her the pictures Portia had just given me.

She looked at her phone for a moment as Ginger was calling our meeting to order. A small smile touched her lips, and I had to force myself to look away. No one cared about us, except for maybe Ginger, but I felt like every time I even thought about her, I was giving myself away.

My phone vibrated again. I looked down and immediately slammed the screen against my chest. I shot daggers at Tokyo who had the nerve to look off in the distance like she hadn't just sent me a picture of the two of us sitting on the floor at Moreland's. We were both smiling, but her hand was definitely inside those bloomers. I risked another glance at the image and quickly saved it. I wondered who took it. I wanted to thank them.

"I'm going to let Camila explain what's going on. I think it's going to make things worse if I do the talking," Ginger said.

"I doubt that, Red, but here we go. There is no easy or good way to say this so I'll just lay it out there. There is something, we'll call it a demon, an evil entity that appears to be targeting our feeders. And when I mean our feeders, I mean feeders from different campuses." Camila went on to explain that two students had been kidnapped and possessed in the last few weeks. One had survived. The other hadn't.

"Whatever these things are, they seem to be determined and on the move. If they decide to try this campus, you girls and our boys across the street, we want you to be ready."

Ginger seemed to find her voice again. "They've been attacking during the day so it makes it difficult for us to track them, but we think if you all are together—"

"What, like all the time?" Chelsea asked.

"Yes, all the time."

That sent a collective groan around the room. Nobody wanted that.

"Girls, please," Omi said. "Let them finish."

"We're trying our best to figure out what's going on, but we can't say the coast is clear until we do, and until then we want you all to keep an eye on each other."

"So if I go on a date with my man, one of the girls has to come with me?" Portia asked.

"I know it's not ideal, but the young man who was killed was picked up by his parents. They could be using people you trust to lure you away from campus."

"Better watch out for your new girlfriend, Jill. She might be possessed—"

"Hollis!" Ginger's voice made us all jump. "Cut the shit! This is not funny!"

"Sorry."

"This thing is trying to get to something, to someone, and I'm pretty sure it's not stopping until it does. I'll be damned if it takes one of you with it." Ginger was practically shaking. I felt bad for being so angry with her. She was *always* trying to protect us.

"Check your e-mail right after we end here," Camila said. "Natasha and Rodrick have worked out who you should be with and when. We're including the boys too. Walk to classes in groups or at least in pairs, and if you have night engagements, one of us is coming with you."

No one seemed pleased, there was still some grumbling, but we understood. I was appropriately afraid.

"That's it for now. When we know more you'll know more," Camila said.

That ended our impromptu get-together. Some of the girls stormed off in a huff. I had some easy assignments to get out of the way, and I wanted to chat with Brayley about our plan for the week, but I texted James first.

Walking buddies?

I stopped by the kitchen for something to drink and munch on while I worked. On my way upstairs my phone vibrated with his text back.

Yeah, LOL Walking buddies.

❖

The way things were going, I expected to be up to the wee hours waiting for a text from Tokyo telling me that she was caught up doing something for the house, or for Dalhem. I couldn't be even the slightest bit upset. Something was trying to kill us. Or possess us to make us do their bidding, whatever that might be.

But not even ten minutes after Portia hopped into bed, Tokyo sent me a text saying she would be up to see me in just a moment.

I started to put away my books, too distracted to study, too worried, nervous, horny, anxious, you name it, to even bother.

Tokyo appeared before I'd even zipped up my book bag. She looked nice fully dressed. Tight black jeans, tiny black crop top. Shiny black boots.

"Finish up already?"

I pressed my finger to my lips. Then pointed to Portia. "She just went to sleep."

"I know. She'll be out until morning."

"What did you do?"

"Nothing, I just cleared her mind. She was stressing out about not being able to be alone with her boyfriend. You'd be surprised how well you sleep when you're not stressed out."

"Gosh, vampires."

"That's me," she said with a smile and a shrug. "Come on. Let's get you between the sheets." She grabbed my covers and pulled them back for me. I wasn't ready for bed, but I had changed. It wouldn't hurt to try to take my mind off things for a while. A few minutes later, I was all changed for bed and was bundled up under my blankets. Tokyo pulled off her boots and climbed in bed with me.

"Weird day, huh?"

"Yes, quite."

"What is really the problem between you and Ginger? I don't understand why she's always mad at you."

"I think it's a few things. She's super tense all of the time 'cause she's like fifteen years old and Dalhem put all these lives in her hands. Omi and them don't take her authority outside of the house that seriously, but they respect her inside the house."

"And you don't?"

"It's not that I don't—Camila and I had our problems before Ginger came on the scene, but we also had this really great understanding. We were really close, all of us, closer than we are now."

I had to wonder what she meant by "close." "Did you and Camila used to sleep together?"

"Let's just put it this way, there is not a vampire you know who hasn't had sex with me or Camila, or Omi, or Natasha, or Faeth. I mean Natasha and Omi are both very committed to Rodrick and Mary, but I don't know, maybe it's an age thing. Things change after forty, fifty, or in Omi's case, a hundred years of not aging or having to do stuff like raise kids. There's a lot of sex to be had."

"And Ginger doesn't like that?"

"I don't think Ginger fully understands it, but I wasn't going to change my whole life because of Ginger, especially when it comes to things that aren't hurting anyone. We all have lives outside of the house, but she acts like what she values is what should be the most important to all of us. I'm just the only one who's vocal in disagreeing with her. Like all the time."

"Hmm."

"Yeah, it's changed the dynamic around here a lot. It's okay."

"Things change."

"They do."

"For example, look how things changed for us."

Tokyo moved closer and kissed my face. "Did you have fun last night?"

"I did. Are you still pretending?"

She shook her head. "No, I'm not."

"Neither am I."

"Are you okay with that? I know this wasn't a part of your plan. I don't want to screw up your science experiment."

"I think my plan was to let things develop naturally. It just so happens that you and I naturally…"

"Like each other? Maybe even love each other a little?"

I nodded as she fiddled with my necklace. I couldn't say it. I'd had strong feelings before, but this was different. With Ginger, I didn't have a choice. With Benny, I was young and foolish, a little desperate. But with Tokyo, my emotions felt real. I didn't know my body could run hot all over just from the thought of seeing someone. I didn't know my stomach could actually tighten and tense all on its own at someone's touch. I had no idea what to do.

"I know it's scary, but it's okay to love people."

"I know it is, but—" I reached down and grabbed her hand, pressed it to my heart. "Do you feel that?"

"Feel it? I could hear it down the hallway."

"No jokes. Really. Do you feel how hard my heart is beating?"

"Yeah, I do."

"This is what happens when I get excited about things. And when I get excited about things I always ruin them."

"No, you don't. You're just surrounded by people who don't know how to be excited with you. They make you feel like you're ruining things when really you're just excited. I like your enthusiasm, Jill. Your passion, because it's real. You're so analytical, but that means when you're ready to get excited about something you know exactly what it means and you know it's exactly what you want."

"It sounds different when you put it that way."

"That's the thing that sucks about being stuck in a nest or a sorority house. You're forced to deal with the people you've been placed with, whether you like them or not, but when you're alone, or at least when you're free, you get to choose. And I love the people I've chosen to be in my life."

"I want to meet more of those people. I want to get to know you, not Bridgette."

"We can do that. Luckily, Camila and Ginger only hate one of my friends."

"I don't care what they think."

"And I love that about you too."

"Thanks for the picture."

"From last night? I thought it was a pretty great shot."

"It was. How long can you stay?"

"Barring major catastrophe, until you get up for class."

"I'm walking to my first two classes with James and Josh, but Hollis and Skylar are in our walking group."

"I saw that. Just don't talk to them. Talk to James. Or daydream about me."

"That won't be hard, but you have to tell me one thing first."

"My real name is Miyoko. About twenty years ago, I had a feeder who went through this phase of calling everyone by where they were from. I've never even lived in Tokyo, but I didn't correct him, and it just stuck."

"Where are you from?"

"Nagasaki."

My stomach dropped as I did the mental math. The shock must have been plain on my face 'cause Tokyo smiled and wrapped her arm around my waist. "I'll tell you about it some other time, okay?"

"Okay. I think we should have sex. Since you're here and demons are out to get us humans."

"Nothing's going to get you, but I'll take your desperate logic as a clear invite."

It took a little shuffling, but she took her jeans off without leaving the bed. My pajama shorts and underwear weren't far behind, and then we were kissing. And then she was kissing my breasts. I never knew how sensitive my nipples were until Tokyo gently toyed with them. Just the tips of her fangs scraping across my skin. Her perfect tongue teasing and teasing.

I wanted her inside me, but I had to work up the courage to say the words.

"Fingers or something more?" she asked when I finally got the words out.

"What does that entail exactly?"

"I can shapeshift specific body parts."

"So you can grow a penis."

"Or just make my clit big enough to penetrate you." She leaned down and licked my lips. "It's up to you."

I watched her mouth, wanting her to lick me again, but I think she was holding back until I made a decision first.

"Fingers first. Magic clit later."

"Sounds good to me. Put your hands above your head."

I followed her instructions and tried to remember to breathe as she climbed over me and gripped my wrists in her hand, pinning them to the bed.

"Does that hurt?"

"Yes," I said honestly. "But I like it." There was too much pressure or maybe just enough, but I didn't want her to let me go.

"Already a perfect little submissive and you didn't even know it."

My response died on my lips, turning into a desperate moan and she slid two fingers inside me. I was already so wet, primed and ready, I squirmed uncontrollably, chasing the friction that I knew would make me come. But she shhh'd me. Told me to calm down, stopped the movements of her fingers and her palm against my clit. Told me to hold on, she would get me there soon enough.

She moved a little more, still gripping my hands above me, still holding me in the grip of her other hand, but moved so her naked body was more firmly pressed against me. I could feel her wetness glide against my hips, feel her own sounds of pleasure vibrate against my bones.

And then she started to move,

Later, after I fell asleep in her arms and even later after she was gone and I stood alone under the hot spray of the shower, I could still feel her, hours later, my body still throbbed for her and I knew I was in trouble. Completely ruined. I couldn't think about class, my project, or even this dark cloud of demon related danger looming over our heads. I just wanted Tokyo, all the time. I wanted her to touch me.

The week that followed was an absolute disaster. We had all grown so used to our routines and our true purpose for being in Alpha Beta Omega, that the second we were forced to spend time with people outside our own little cliques and clusters, I had to start wondering if *anyone* in my sorority or our brother fraternity even liked each other. I almost got in two fights with Hollis after she asked Van when he was going to come out to his parents.

When she asked James if he was going to come out before the draft, in front of his brother, I had to keep James from killing her. Walking to class with Hollis lasted all of two days. I politely asked Ginger if she could walk with just Skylar, and she thought that was okay. It was a little awkward purposefully walking fifty yards behind them. But I couldn't force myself to deal with more of what Hollis considered small talk.

Things with Ginger hadn't gotten any better either. She wasn't mean to me or anything, but she was just...bitter maybe. Or pissed. I had to chalk it up to our blood bond and the possessive jealousy it bred. I understood. A possessive vampire meant their humans were safe. I couldn't imagine being bound to a vampire who didn't give a care about me or what I did or who I was with. But in the end, it really just felt like some petty middle school drama.

Tokyo had my attention and Ginger simply didn't like it, but I didn't care. When I saw Ginger again, to talk about maiming Hollis, she agreed that she wouldn't tell the girls, had already made that decision not to say anything based on the sheer fact that Tokyo's feeders were just as possessive as her, and would throw a minor tantrum if they knew their sister-queen was carrying on a full romantic relationship with a human she had no blood claims to right under their noses. D'Monique and Chelsea knew how to argue, and I was no match for them.

Wednesday, I asked Ava to hand out some surveys at the University Greek Association meeting. I only got about half of the surveys back and half of those were filled with joke answers like *"Just how illegal is bestiality?"* and *"In how many states can I give it to Phil's mom?"* Brayley had hit some roadblocks too. Her English professor changed his mind and wouldn't let their class fill out our "sex survey." It was apparently rude and improper, and he didn't want to be reprimanded by the chancellor's office if any parents found out. She had better luck in her astronomy lecture, but still I felt we were thousands of samples short.

Thursday, while I was waiting for Taylor to get her HRT shot so we could walk to class together, Beth sent me a text saying that she was leaving without us to walk with one of the guys from OBA. Turns out she just went by herself to campus and she, Taylor, and I all got chewed out for not being more vigilant. I kept my comments to Beth to myself, but Taylor let her have it and rightfully so.

I saw Tokyo whenever I could, but the tension in the house was so high, every second we got together was spent rehashing whatever drama had unfolded while we'd been apart. Portia and her boyfriend were fighting so she was wonderful to be around, when she wasn't crying. Yazmeen got jealous that the walking schedule had Kait spending way more time with Tierra. I didn't even know Yazmeen and Kait were a thing, but that all came out in front of everyone Thursday night while we were trying to watch TV.

I heard a rumor that Camila and Ginger were thinking about cancelling the Friday night movie night just to give us a break from each other, but that was just a rumor. I went down and gave my blood donation and went right back up to my room. Three other girls followed me. Yeah, things were not good. I didn't see Tokyo at all that night, but I woke up to a text from her, and more flowers.

Tonight, just me and you.
I made reservations of sorts.
Dress comfortably.
I had never been so relieved to receive a text in my life.

CHAPTER FIFTEEN

Jill

Tokyo was picking me up at eight. Most of the girls were getting ready to go out to another party on the Row. The rest had picked their factions and taken up residence with their sister-queens or in front of various screens around the house. I was ready to get the heck out of there. Portia was still fighting with her boyfriend so I didn't say anything about having a date while I was getting ready, but she guessed that I was headed out with Bridgette and insisted on giving me pointers on what to do with my hair even though I was just settling on a bun.

I needed some alone time with Tokyo. And some sex. I didn't care what my hair looked like. I ignored her too when she had something to say about the jeans and sneakers I was wearing. I grabbed my jacket and walked out of the room before she could dispense any more of her opinions. I really hoped our sister-queens figured out this evil demon problem soon. I didn't think our peaceful slice of Greekdom could handle much more infighting.

Tokyo showed up right on time, as Bridgette just in case anyone saw her. I didn't even bother telling the girls where I was going or asking one of them to come along. I'd lied and told

Portia we were going to the movies and James was coming with us.

When I climbed in the car, I sent Ginger a text.

Going out with Miyoko.

I'll check in at nine. Be back by two.

Her response was immediate and approximately fifty percent sincere.

Have fun and call me if you need a ride.

"Are you two okay?" I asked Tokyo as we drove away from the house. "You and Ginger? She's never really completely mad at me, but I don't like the idea of her being upset with you because of me."

She reached over and took my hand. "Don't worry about me and Ginger. Without a time machine, there's no way to fix this. Even if we stopped seeing each other now, she would be pissed that we were together at all, and then when she got over that, she'd find some other reason to be pissed off at me. The end."

"Well, that makes me upset. I…I don't like the idea of people not liking you."

"That's very sweet."

"Where are you taking me this time?"

"Sex dungeon. I was going to tie you up and then let a bunch of vampires tickle you with feathers while I fuck you from behind."

"That sounds more weird than sexy."

"No, I'm taking you to my place."

"You have another house?"

"Yup, I have several, but this is my primary, well, main secondary residence for now. I have a vacant place in Los Angeles and just outside of San Francisco, and feeders living in my other houses around our territory."

"So you can only live in Dalhem's zone or whatever it's called?"

"Yeah, we can go anywhere we want, but we have to let the governing authority, so to speak, know that we are coming to visit. They don't like random vampires walking among their human population unsupervised."

"It makes sense."

"Trust me, it does. Not all of us are as kind and sweet as me and my sister-queens." It wasn't hard for me to believe her.

We drove for thirty minutes or so to a cute neighborhood on the water. Tokyo stopped at a larger, newly remodeled house, gray with white shutters. I followed her inside, taking in my surroundings as the lights flicked on as we moved deeper and deeper into the house. It looked like it was straight out of a design catalog, the perfect harbor home with perfect beach decor. The place was little and inviting. So different from the dark cave Tokyo called home under the ABO house.

We walked into the kitchen, my dream kitchen, and I almost fainted. Large counter. Double ovens. Huge sink. And she had every tool I needed to make my favorite desserts right out on the counter. I just needed some ingredients.

"Dinner is on its way, and I was hoping you would make dessert."

"I'd love to." I pulled off my coat and tore open the fridge only to find it completely empty.

"I don't keep food here."

"Of course, um, should we go to the store or do we have to wait for the food?"

"Tell me exactly what you need." She handed me a pad of paper. Actually, it was stationery, fancy white stationery with two blue crabs and the initials MH at the top. Who was this woman?

I wrote down everything I needed for the mixed berry lemon bars I loved to make with Dad, and since there was another oven, everything I needed for my cream-filled red velvet cupcakes.

"This is a hefty list. So I'll poof out to the store. Shouldn't be gone more than five."

"And what if I'm kidnapped and possessed while you're gone?"

"That's why I'm not leaving you alone. There's someone I want you to meet."

A beautiful black woman appeared in the kitchen. She was dressed like a fifties starlet. Her hair was styled in elegant curls, but she was wearing pedal pushers and an oversized men's button down. She had simple blue Keds on her feet. Her smile was pure warmth. And so were her wide brown eyes.

"Jill, this is Henrietta Whitfield. Hattie for short. Hattie's my primary. She's my maker."

I tried to process that little bit of news with the dots my mind was suddenly connecting. That's why she looked so familiar. Hattie Whitfield was the most famous black actress of the sixties, made even more famous by her early death during a motorcycle accident. The scandal was made even more scandalous because her lover at the wheel was her white, very married co-star.

"It's lovely to meet you, Jill."

"Likewise."

"I'll be right back, Jill. I gave Hattie permission to spill all my business so ask away." She kissed me on my cheek and then she vanished.

I had no idea what to say.

"Miyoko must like you an awful lot. I've only met a few girls from the house before." She hadn't been in a film in almost fifty years, but she still sounded like a movie star. She oozed charisma.

"I think we got together under strange circumstances."

"Didn't we all. Do you drink?"

"Some."

"Well, with that accent you can't be a stranger to wine. I'll get you a glass."

"Thank you." I stood by the counter and accepted the healthy glass of Merlot she poured me. Then she hopped up on the marble surface and seemed to settle in for a chat.

"So you belong to Ginger, but you and Miyoko are falling in love?"

"Yes, that seems to be the case."

"I hate to play favorites. I have several who share my bloodline, but Miyoko is my favorite. She's very special to me."

"Erm—how did you two meet?"

"The same way most vampires meet their maker. Miyoko almost died."

"During World War II?"

"Because of World War II. After they dropped the bombs, Paneo filled a plane with survivors and vampires to keep them alive during their journey, and sent them here to the U.S. They were made comfortable, but she wanted the government to see exactly what they had done. The regular civilians, children, grandparents, hardworking men and women who had nothing to do with the conflict.

"The lives they'd destroyed. The men responsible...let's just say the response was despicable. The survivors Dalhem was able to save from the government facilities were given a choice, a painless death or they could be made into one of us. Miyoko chose to be one of us."

"And the ones he wasn't able to save?

"Some died, even with the help of our blood. They were too badly injured. And the others...they did not make it back to Japan." Years had passed, but I could see the blue tears lining Hattie's eyes. A knot tied in my own throat. I reached for a paper towel near the sink and handed it to her.

"Thank you. Many governments make it a business to hide the depths of their atrocities. The reason she's okay with me telling you about her life and her past is because she doesn't remember.

The days leading up to her rebirth were so traumatic, Dalhem and I had to help her shield her mind so she could go on living."

It made sense. I'd heard of the minds of victims of trauma doing extraordinary things to protect them from the horrors of their reality. I couldn't imagine what it would be like to survive an atomic blast.

"How old was Tokyo when this happened? I mean Miyoko."

Hattie smiled and squeezed my hand. "She likes both names just fine. She had just celebrated her eightieth birthday, but after her rebirth, I had a teenager on my hands. We helped her hold on to certain memories, good memories and some bad, the pieces that made her who she was, but she pushed a lot of that away to make room for the present, I think."

"What'd I miss?" I almost spilled my wine when Tokyo reappeared right in front of the fridge, her arms loaded down with groceries.

"Here, let me help you." I reached for the bags, but she nudged me away with her hip.

"You get the door." Of course the doorbell rang. I ran to go get it realizing I didn't have any cash to tip the driver.

"Tip's included!" Tokyo yelled after me before I could turn around.

I returned to the kitchen and placed dinner on the center island while Tokyo was busy setting out my baking ingredients on the other counter.

"We were just talking about you. Your life, before and after."

"Oh, yeah." Tokyo looked over her shoulder at me. "I have PTSD wicked bad, but it's been a nice little do over. Got to pick the bod I wanted. People forever think I'm twenty-five. I've got young college coeds hanging all over me. I think I'm doing all right. What do you think, Hattie?" My heart was pounding, but her laugh made me smile through the tears I could feel clouding my eyes.

"You're doing great and you always have," Hattie said. I was instantly pissed at Ginger. Tokyo lived her life the way that was best for her, a way that made her happy, and Ginger or Camila had no right—

Tokyo was in front of me taking my hands. "Hey, are you okay?" She reached up and wiped an errant tear from my face.

"Yes. I'm sorry. I'm fine." I shook my head, wiping my face again. She was fine. She was here, alive, with me. I didn't know why I was so upset.

"I know this stuff is kind of heavy."

"It is; it's just—never mind."

"Miyoko tells me you're an amazing baker."

"Yes," I said. That brought back a genuine smile. "And I can eat and bake at the same time so if you don't mind spoon feeding me, I'll preheat these ovens and get going."

"Hattie, you're seriously gonna die. Her desserts are the best."

Hattie laughed and poured herself more wine. "What a lovely way to go."

❖

Hattie stayed until all the baking was done, and we'd demolished the Italian food Tokyo had ordered for us. Sometime during my second glass of wine, I started to relax, started to forget about Ginger and the stick up her butt, and started to enjoy myself. Hattie was wonderful. Funny and kind. I loved the way she looked at Tokyo, like she was so proud and just happy to be around her. And not once did I think that genuine affection was due to their blood bond. I think if Hattie and Tokyo had to sever all their supernatural ties that night, Hattie would still care about Tokyo and Tokyo would feel the same. They would remain friends.

Around 11:30, Hattie left, but not without vanishing with a large plastic ware tub filled with cupcakes and mixed berry lemon bars. She told me if I was ever in San Francisco, I was more than welcome to come stay with her. Or bake for her.

When she left, I tried to start cleaning up, but Tokyo had other plans.

She came up behind while I was suds deep in the sink.

"I can do that later," she said, rubbing the back of my neck. She was at her full height and she had to bend to kiss me in the tender spot. I knew she'd shrink down if I asked her to, but if this was her natural form, then that's how I wanted her.

"My dad and papa would kill me if they knew I was leaving dirty dishes behind."

"How about I don't tell them and you come over here and let me fuck you like I've been wanting to do all night." She reached around me and turned off the water. I continued to hold still as she reached for the dish towel and dried my hands.

"Am I being instructed to let you have sex with me or do you have to ask me nicely?"

Tokyo didn't answer. She spun me around and picked me up by my bottom. And then her lips were on mine. And then I was on the center island.

"Do you want me to ask you nicely?"

I shook my head. "I think you already know what I want."

"Do I?"

"Hmmm."

"Should I make you say it?"

I took a deep breath and gave the whole dirty talk thing a try. "I…would like you to fuck me. Right now. With your magic shape-shifting clit. Please."

"Aww, baby. You did it."

"I'm growing stronger every day," I said, trying to keep a straight face. "It's the power of love."

Tokyo wasn't so successful. She tried to cover her snort of laughter, but failed. "Lean back." I propped myself up, giving her just enough room to unzip my jeans and pull them down. As soon as they were off, I nearly lunged forward so I could kiss her again. I had the silly thought, if it were possible, we would be kissing all the time. She held me close, giving me what I wanted, bit by bit, but not fast enough. I wanted her inside me now.

"I know, baby. I don't want to hurt you."

"You know what?" I moaned as her fingers grazed my clit.

"How bad you want me. I want you too." Her arm moved down to my waist, and she pulled me closer to the edge of the counter. "Guide me in."

"What?"

She looked down between us. I followed her gaze down and saw what she was talking about. Her clit had extended and thickened into a decent sized phallus. With a little help, she wrapped my fingers around its girth. It was wet, covered in her juices, so potent I could smell her. My mouth started to water.

"How does that feel?"

"Good, baby. Let me in."

"Tell me if I'm doing it wrong."

"I will and you won't."

I stroked my hand up and down the length of her clit for just a moment, watched her eyes close and the pleasure wash over her. If I had any confidence in my oral skills, I would have asked if I could go down on her.

"Do you want me to fuck your mouth first?"

"How did you know what I wanted?"

"I don't know. For some reason, you're in my head."

"I am?"

"Yeah. If you keep doing that I'm gonna come." My hand was still moving. "It's fine. I'll come again, but if you want this first one to be in your mouth, you're gonna have to back off a bit, baby. Oh fuck." Her fangs dug into her bottom lip as she leaned into me.

I had so many questions, but her pleasure was all I could think of and I did want her in my mouth, and…I nudged her back and hopped off the counter. I used my jeans to cushion my knees. A moment later, her fingers were in my hair pulling my head back. I knew she could be gentle, she was always gentle, but that wasn't what I wanted and that's not what she gave me. She teased me a moment, using the tip of her engorged clit to rub her juices all over my lips. That only lasted a moment.

"Open, and breathe through your nose."

As I did, she shoved her clit into my mouth. It felt strange, how much I enjoyed it, how much I didn't want her to stop. She pumped in and out, and I knew at some point I should close my mouth just a little bit to create some suction. So I'd heard.

Tokyo groaned out a "Fuuuuck," and gripped the counter. I tried to suck a little harder going against the motion of her hips, but when I glanced up for any sign or any cue that I was doing anything right or wrong, she was shaking her head. "Here." Tokyo squatted in front of me and tore my shirt over my head. She popped the hook on my bra and pulled that off just as quickly, and there I was completely naked before her, counting the seconds before she was back in my mouth.

"You were gagging a little bit. Breathe through your nose, but don't try to swallow. Just let it run out of your mouth."

"Okay," I gasped before she shoved her way back in. I don't know why, but her roughness was turning me on so much. Maybe it was all the built up tension and stress from the week. Maybe it was all the pent up emotion from meeting Hattie and listening to her speak so lovingly about Tokyo. Or maybe it was the fact that we had barely gotten to screw during the week. Just two perfect, yet quiet and extremely gentle encounters. I wanted the reckless excitement I'd experienced at Moreland's party. The chase, the seemingly high stakes. Maybe a bit of the humiliation.

"Oh fuck! Please don't say that." She was purring now, almost growling, barely able to control the true animal that lived inside her.

Well, right, she was in my head. Then she had to know how much I was enjoying this, my drool mixed with her juices dribbling all over my chest. She had to know how badly I wanted to finger myself, but I didn't dare because I liked the way my nails felt gripping her thighs. She had to know how I thought maybe I might come just from the way my hips were rocking so close to the floor. The muscles of my vagina tensing over and over.

"Next time, we'll get you an audience. Would you like that?"

I hated having sex in front of the girls. When we weren't naked, they were always making fun of me, but I didn't feel that way with Krystal and Moreland and Luke. Even Mayor Fillamorrow, who clearly knew how to let her hair down. I felt welcomed by them, comfortable in their company, like I could do anything with them around and they wouldn't tease me or make me feel like I was too enthusiastic about Tokyo and the amazing things she could do to me.

"Well, we'll have to make that happen. I'll fuck your mouth and your tight pussy in front of Moreland and all her friends. You'd like that."

I nodded my agreement, moaning with my full mouth.

Tokyo's clit just seemed to get wetter and wetter. My drool began to run out of my mouth. The feel of it was making my body more and more sensitive. If Tokyo didn't do something soon I was worried I would explode.

"We can't have that." She slipped out of my mouth as she dropped to her knees in front of me. "You should see how fucking hot you look right now. I don't even want to touch you. I love how desperate you are."

"Please," I practically whimpered. On its own, my hand reached up and started spreading the drool around my nipples.

"Say it again."

"Please."

"God, there are so many things I want to put in your mouth. Come here." She leaned back against the cabinets and pulled me onto her lap. She reached down between my legs, placing herself at my very swollen, very ready entrance. All I had to do was sit. And not far either, when her perfectly sized length filled me up. Goodness, how good she felt.

I'd never ridden a clit like that before, with Tokyo guiding my hips and sucking on my nipples, I managed to get the hang of it. I came so loud I'm pretty sure her neighbors heard my screams.

❖

Once I got a clear understanding of how it was actually possible to screw all over one's kitchen, Tokyo drove me home. I was too high, too perfectly sated to care about the freezing temperatures outside or the still bizarre mood in the house. It was late, but almost everyone was still up and in awful moods. A hot shower helped me get my wits back, but only a little. I couldn't stop touching myself under the spray.

Portia sitting in the hallway sweet-talking with her boyfriend helped make room for some clarity though. After I dressed for bed, I noticed a stack of blank surveys on my desk. I picked one up and grabbed a pen. I had a girlfriend now, a real one, and there was definitely sexual activity, but still there were so many things I didn't have to worry about due to the simple fact that she wasn't human. Maybe that would make me careless.

I checked off the box for STD prevention, and I never knew what the future held or how far things could go…with an audience, so I checked off the box for birth control too. There was also a box marked *relationships*, and because I'm also practical and forward thinking, I had to be realistic and know that it was perfectly reasonable for me to write "how to handle a breakup" in that empty space.

I was most certainly in love now, and I had every reason to be terrified that things with my real, undead girlfriend might not last forever.

As if she could sense the downturn in my mood, my phone vibrated with a text from Tokyo.

It was a very graphic picture of her wet fingers between her legs.

I know it's not a tasteful nude, but I don't care.

I'm still thinking about you.

That was enough to give me sweet dreams for the whole night.

CHAPTER SIXTEEN

Tokyo

I'd gone from undead babysitter on house arrest to undead demon detective in a matter of weeks. When I wasn't with the girls or Jill, I was hitting every police station, every sheriff's office and highway patrol stop between Baltimore, Durham, and Austin. And nothing. No leads. The only clear victims I could find belonged to the vampires and our nests. I hit a few of the unloyals, vampires who agreed in the loosest terms to Dalhem's laws, but did not serve him or any other demon-borne. He allowed them to live within his borders as long as they cleaned up after their feedings and never, ever left any bodies behind. Some of them had bound feeders, but the ones I caught up with hadn't heard anything. Their feeders were safe and sound.

So far, the only lead was that the thing was moving.

The day we got a call from the Lambda chapter up at UNY, Ginger and Dalhem agreed that I should go talk to the girl in person, then speak to any of the locals who might know something.

I went up as soon as the sun was down and met with the head sister-queen, Lila.

Lila brought me to her underground dwelling, where Rory, a junior from Long Island, was visibly shaken.

"Rory, this is Miyoko. She's from the Alpha nest. They're trying to make sure no one gets snatched up again."

"It's nice to meet you, Rory," I said, trying to keep her calm. Her eyes were darting all over the place. "I heard you put up one hell of a fight."

Rory nodded, and I thought she was about to bite through her lip.

"Can you tell me what happened?"

"I was with Antonia, my roommate, and we were going to check out this free concert down at the park after class. And Mario, the guy I sit next to in my engineering lab, he wanted to come.

"Where's Antonia?" I asked Lila. "Get her down here now."

"I thought it was fine because Lila told us to stick together. I had Antonia with me. We were looking out for each other. Except when we got to the park, there was a huge crowd and things were getting out of control. People were shoving, and the cops came, which never helps. So Antonia said we should leave."

Just then a Latin girl, about medium everything with braces, cracked open the door. Lila waved her in.

"I'm just telling them what happened," Rory said.

"Yeah, it was really fucked up. I mean screwed up. Sorry."

"It's okay. You can swear all you want. Tell me what happened next."

"The cops were trying to direct people and we got separated, and it was only for like a minute, but Mario started dragging me away. Like not trying to get me out of the way, but like he was trying to take me somewhere and we were headed in the opposite direction of school.

"I started fighting him, and he looked at me and something was way fucked with his eyes, like his eyes turned this really creepy gray and then my hand started to hurt." She held out her palm for me. Her fingers were still a little red like they'd been squeezed too hard. But I was more concerned about the gray blotch in the center of her palm. All our Masters had a mark. Dalhem's was a six-pointed star made out of six overlapping orbs. At a glance, it almost looked like a flower. This thing was unrecognizable, but it was something.

With her permission, I snapped a picture and sent it to Dalhem.

"Thank you. Please go on."

"My hand started hurting, and then I got this weird taste in my mouth, like how firewood smells, but the wood's got rotten garbage on it. That's what it tasted like. I blacked out for...I don't know how long it was, but I wasn't completely out. I could still hear, and I could feel everything. I just couldn't talk and I couldn't see."

"I found Mario trying to drag her behind some boulders in the park," Antonia went on. "And it was his eyes like Rory said, but when I saw her face, her eyes were starting to change too. I knew it wasn't just regular bad, you know."

I nodded, not wanting to interrupt.

"I ran up after them and when I grabbed Rory, she and Mario said..."

Antonia was visibly shaking now.

"Please. It's okay. What did it say?"

"Bring me to your Master," both girls said at once.

"So I just started praying, well, kinda. This thing I know."

"Tell me exactly what you said."

Antonia repeated the words that quite possibly saved Rory and Mario's lives, but it was no prayer. It was hard for me not to grab her by the shoulders and shake her. I glanced at Lila. She looked like she was about to vomit.

"Where did you learn that? Who taught that to you?"

"My aunt," Antonia said. "She told me to say it if I ever get a bad feeling. She said it banishes evil." Well, the woman wasn't wrong. Hattie had taught the so-called prayer to me years ago. A lot of us vampires knew it. Except it wasn't a prayer. It was a protection spell in a dialect of Aramaic. In my whole life as a demon-reborn, I never once had to use it and for that exact reason I'd forgotten about it. That was the thing about preventative measures. They always seemed to come in handy after the fact. Necessity sure did change things.

"Is your aunt blood bound? Who does she feed?"

"No one. She just…believes."

That was the tricky thing about real evil, and even real good. They transcended all human understanding, all religious boundaries, but you'd be surprised how much better equipped you could be to deal with them just by believing. Humility got you a long way too.

"So what happened after that?"

"The thing, whatever it was, just vanished, but Rory and Mario were super freaked out. So I got them to a cab and we came back."

"You did a really good job, Antonia. Thank you."

"No problem. I'm still kinda freaked out."

"I know. So am I." I turned to Lila. "Where's Mario?"

"I took care of him and sent him back to his dorm." By took care of him she meant wiped his memory, which was the exact right thing to do.

"Okay, well, girls, Lila and I are going to put you to sleep for just a minute if that's okay. We're just going to peek at your memories, get rid of the stuff about today that will traumatize you forever, but leave good information for you to recall when you need your survival instincts to kick in. How does that sound?"

"Perfect."

"Fucking great. Please do it."

Their enthusiasm at being essentially brainwashed made me laugh a little. We had them both move to Lila's bedroom where she put them both to sleep. Then I dove into their memories extracting everything, every sight, sound, smell that they'd captured that afternoon. They'd both given extremely accurate accounts. The huge crowd, the cops, the gray of Mario's eyes, and even that taste Rory had described, like rotten garbage and firewood. And that ominous message.

I could hear the creature's voice plain and clear. It wanted to speak to Dalhem.

❖

I didn't head straight back to the house. I went to Dalhem's instead. I felt bad and sufficiently stupid for showing up when I did. It was family time. Benny and Cleo, Dalhem and his wife/ Benny's mom, Leanne, all gathered around watching J.J. power crawl across the floor.

I had no idea why Dalhem had invited me into their living quarters and not his office, but whatever. I sat there for a few awkward minutes, answering softball questions about the girls and pretending to be interested in J.J.'s development. I mean I was concerned about the kid's general well-being, but Dalhem's house was the safest place on the planet, and J.J. wasn't going to help us solve this little mystery.

"I'm hoping to get a 'Mama' soon, but so far just really expressive noises. Isn't that right, baby?" Benny said.

"She's so cute," I said as J.J. sat back on her cushy butt and waved a stuffed turtle at me. I really needed to get back to the house.

"I will step into the office with my Miyoko. My Cleo will join us."

"Okay," Benny said with a smile.

"Tokyo, don't be a stranger. You and your sister-queens are welcome here anytime," Leanne offered.

"Thank you," I said, knowing full well there would be no social visits without the rest of my sister-queens. The whole "I used to fuck your daughter's wife" thing was too much.

Dalhem gestured for us to lead the way out of the room, on foot. We barely made it out the door before J.J. started screaming bloody murder. Dalhem immediately turned around and scooped her up. That shut her right up.

But not her mom. "So you're dating Jill now," Cleo said. Camila and Ginger really couldn't mind their own business.

"I am, but can we not. It just happened and it's been pretty good. You don't need to shit on—"

"Hey, whoa. That's not what I was going to say at all. I was just asking."

"Well, yeah. We're dating."

"That's cool. And it wasn't Ginger or Camila who told me. Faeth's your fink, and she actually told me you and Jill are really good together. But you're keeping it secret from the girls."

"Just thought it would be easier. A lot of opinions in that house."

"No, you're right. Why do you think I left?"

I looked over at Cleo's raised eyebrow. I thought Benny had made her leave, but maybe I had gotten that all wrong.

Cleo opened Dalhem's office door for us. "I just want you to be happy. I mean that."

"Thank you."

We took a seat on Dalhem's gaudy gold and mahogany furniture.

"This demon, it seeks me out," he said.

"Yes, uh, you saw the picture I sent over, and here." He took my outstretched hand and instantly absorbed all of Rory and Antonia's memories. Then he passed them to Cleo, probably with his own footnotes.

"I will send a message to my sister. We all thank you," he said, bouncing J.J. in his arms.

"That's it? You don't want me to do anything else?"

"I want you to continue with eyes open, my Miyoko. I want you to return to my nest and take care of my children. Protect them."

I glanced at Cleo, but her face was expressionless. She was inner circle now, and I was still a worker bee. Dalhem stood and handed the baby back to Cleo. And then he took me. We vanished into the cool night, into the sky, and he held me there, our particles adrift, but my whole being held safely in his hands.

"Never doubt me, my darling."

"There's no doubt. I just want to help."

"And my wish is for you to protect my girls. My wish is for you to be safe. Do you understand?"

I did. I had a feeling I was putting myself in danger by chasing this thing down. It was better for everyone if I kept close to home. Pleased with my acceptance of the truth, I felt Dalhem's arms around me and his lips across my forehead. When I opened my eyes, I was back in my apartment under the ABO house and Dalhem was gone.

❖

After I got back to the house, it only took a couple of hours for Cleo to get the word out about what had happened to Rory and her friends. Ginger wanted to tell the girls and remind them that things might be quiet in our neck of the woods, but whatever this thing was, it had an objective and it wasn't going to stop using our girls until it achieved that goal.

We had a lot of meetings, conversations. I think more than a few of us thought that Dalhem needed to meet this demon head on, but from the way he was acting, it was almost as if he was scared. And that didn't put me at ease, especially when I couldn't stop replaying the horror show I'd pulled from Rory's memory.

This demon was no playful ghost. This thing was head-hunting. What if it didn't want Dalhem? What if he just wanted to talk to him because something worse was coming? What if terrorizing our girls and the OBA boys wasn't even necessary, just some part of the show? What if it slipped by and killed someone else?

I could still feel that thing, smell it, taste it, days later and it scared the shit out of me. I pulled my girls aside separately and stressed to them how important it was for them to keep an eye out for each other. And while they were sleeping, I implanted the protection spell in their memories. I linked it to triggers from Rory's encounter, what she saw, what she tasted. If they ran into that piece of shit, they wouldn't know why, but they would know exactly what to do.

I felt better knowing they had a bit of an edge. I might have passed the suggestion on to Faeth and Kina. And Ginger. She blew me off 'cause she was stressed and not listening and thinking that I wasn't giving good advice 'cause she could trust me with one sixth of her kingdom, but she couldn't take one simple hint based on super fucking reliable information. Maybe Cleo was on to something. Maybe sooner rather than later, it would be time for me to go.

The girls helped me relax, but Jill quickly became my safe harbor. We were spending more and more time together so I had to be a little more deceptive with the girls about how and where I was spending my time. I wasn't always out doing demon recon. A lot of the time I was at the library or in bed with Jill.

I tried not to think too hard on the connections that were starting to form between us. First, the shared orgasms and then the small bits of telepathy that were becoming more and more frequent, and then a few days after the incident with Rory, I started to get a general sense of her moods. None of this should be happening, not unless we were blood bound, and we sure as fuck weren't. But that didn't stop the way she made me feel, and my emotions, my love for her, was only compounded by the overwhelming way she felt for me. And she was happy all the time now, so I could feel that too, and it was the perfect distraction from the absolute shit show that was going on around us.

I decided one night while she was studying in my bed to tell her about the banishment. She was lying over my thighs, her perfect little round ass up in the air. I was doing my best not to distract her, only rubbing her cheeks over her jeans and not fingering her the way she deserved to be for sitting across my lap like that. The movie we were watching ended so I flipped through the guide trying to find more mindless crap to zone out to.

I turned to *The Notebook* like an idiot, one movie you don't watch when you're on an emotional ledge.

"I always cry at the end of this movie. So tragic," Jill muttered absently. She squirmed when I gave her butt a little squeeze.

"At least they die together."

"True."

"Hey, if I teach you something will you do your best to memorize it?"

Jill tapped the side of her head. "Got the whole periodic table up here. What's a bit more information?"

"No, baby. I mean it. It's important."

Jill sat up slowly and turned to face me. She reached up and smoothed some hair away from my face. "What's going on?"

I brought up the Rory situation and then one of a few parts Ginger had purposefully left out during our chat with the group.

"Why don't all the girls know it? I mean shouldn't we all?" she asked.

"I don't know. I'd just—I'd give it to you if I could, but you're still bound to Ginger, and despite however well she's handling us being together, you're still hers and my being inside your head would cross too many lines."

"But I'm yours too." Her thumb drifted down and teased my bottom lip. I slowly licked it then nipped her nail with my fang.

"I know, baby, but I can only push her so far."

"I know." The disappointment on her face pained me to my core.

"This thing, I don't know what tricks it has up its sleeves. I don't know what it'll try next, but if you think you're in danger, just say these words over and over again until you can get away." I spoke the enchantment and made Jill repeat it at least ten times until she had it.

"You think it'll come here?"

"I don't know. That's what scares me. I have no idea. The way it tried to grab Rory out in public like that, maybe it's getting desperate. I just want you to be safe."

"I hate seeing you this upset."

"I'm sorry. Just stressed."

"Well, I think we're safe down here. Is there something we could do about that stress?"

"I think so. But you're a little overdressed."

Jill looked down at herself. "I suppose I am."

"You want some help?"

"That would be helpful, yes."

I pounced on her, throwing her down on my bed on her back. The little squeak she made echoed the thumping of her heart as I made quick work of her jeans and underwear. Her shirt was easy enough, and her bra served as a perfect pair of restraints. You'd be surprised what you could do with some bra straps and some knot tying skills. I stood over her, looking at every inch of her perfect body, from her caramel brown skin to her small, delectable breasts, to the slick cleft between her legs. The ruby around her neck glinted in the light above my bed, and for a moment, I felt the most irrational stab of jealousy. That should be my ruby around her neck, her blood sustaining me.

"Hey. Hey."

"Sorry, what?" I blinked, and it took a second, but I was finally able to focus on her face.

"What's the matter? You were growling, and your eyes were doing that glowy thing."

My fangs were out too, fully extended and ready to tear into the first thing that got into my way. I shook my head and forced my canines back up into my gums.

Jill reached out to me with her bound hands. "Come here."

I pulled off my clothes and joined her on the bed, crawling over her beautiful body. She looped her bound hands over my head and draped her arms around my shoulders, but it wasn't until I felt her lips on my face, slowly caressing my lips, that I was fully under control, my growling subsiding to a more reasonable purr.

"Just be here with me," she whispered.

"I am," I said between kisses. And I always would be.

Chapter Seventeen

Tokyo

The week before the girls left for Thanksgiving break, I decided that I had had enough of the silent peace that Ginger and I had established. And what better way to disturb that peace than by asking her the one thing that was sure to set her right the fuck off. Maybe I was just cagey thinking about what had happened to the girls at UNY. Maybe I was just feeling territorial and uncertain, but I had to do something. The girls were off at class, and I knew Camila was going over the sorority's books. It was the ideal time to ask Ginger to come talk to me. She never came by my place unless I was hosting a sister-queen meeting, so I figured for once she could vanish her ass over to my apartment.

I invited her to sit down, ignoring the way she was eyeing the pillows and mats that made up the sitting area in my TV room like she was afraid she was accidentally going to sit in a pile of jizz. She had just as much sex, if not more, on her own living room furniture. Finally, she sat down cross-legged, but didn't make herself comfortable.

"So what's up?"

"I want Jill."

"Uh, you have her. I sanctioned this little love affair you have going on. Dalhem said it's fine. Not exactly sure what else you could want."

Ginger knew, but she didn't think I was insane enough to say it. So I said it. "I want Jill to feed me. I want to claim her as mine, officially."

Ginger's face turned so red I thought one of her freckles was going to pop off. "Have you claimed her unofficially?"

"You know what I mean. I want Jill to be one of my feeders."

"And I'm saying no. Good talk though." Ginger stood to leave, but I was far from finished.

"You can't force her to stay with you."

"And you can't force me to release her just because you want to enjoy the full sex spectrum with her blood in your system. I said no."

"At least let her choose. I mean it's kinda fucked that we have to decide who the girls feed based on who we want, isn't it? Hell, I wanted you once upon a time."

"Yeah, good thing that didn't work out. My answer is still no."

"Just let me ask her. Let her decide instead of you deciding for her." I pulled out my phone and hit her contact.

Ginger reached for the phone, trying to knock it out of my hand. "What the fuck are you doing?"

"I'm settling this."

"She's in between classes and you're gonna drop this on her?"

I hated to admit that Ginger was right. Too bad Jill answered her phone. "Hey, what's up?"

"She's going to be thinking about this when she should be focused on class," Ginger whisper-shouted, and then she gave me the stank eye when I started speaking French.

"Nothing, I was just calling to hear your voice. I miss you."

"I miss you too. Brayley had a whole stack of surveys, and now she can't find them so that's great. Those were the last ones we had time to collect before we finalize our presentation. I really hope she finds them."

"I'm sure they'll turn up. You want to come see me tonight?"

"Sure, what time? I heard Yaz saying it was her night to feed you."

"How about ten thirty? She usually comes down right after curfew."

"Ten thirty it is." We said our good-byes and then I hung up.

"So at ten thirty you're just gonna ambush her?"

"I'm not gonna ambush her. We're gonna talk and then we'll let you know her decision."

"No. The three of us are going to talk, and Jill will give us both her decision. And that's only if I agree to it. I'm not gonna let you twist and confuse the pros and cons of this situation so you can manipulate her into feeding you."

"This isn't about manipulating anyone. I love her. I want to feed from her. I want her with me."

"Fine, whatever. Ten thirty, and don't call her back and change the time. I'll sense her when she comes down here."

"Will you though?"

"What?"

"Your hold on her is slipping isn't it? I noticed it a few weeks ago. Jill was walking toward your apartment, but you didn't even pick up on her until she was practically walking through your door."

Ginger didn't say anything, but she didn't have to. She knew I was right.

"Have you even noticed how often Jill's been down here? How many nights she's spent in my room? No, 'cause you're telling yourself you've been tuning her out more since we started dating. You don't want to know when we're together, you don't want to know how good I make her feel, but it's because you can barely feel her anymore. It's because she belongs with me. She's already chosen me."

"I really suggest you stop talking right now."

"Or what? Dalhem's not going to let you fuck me up just because I'm telling you something you don't want to hear. You can't control everything, Ginger, and you sure as hell can't protect Jill like I can."

Ginger scoffed at me, actually laughed in my face. "Okay. Whatever you say. And just for the record, I can sense Jill just fine, and if you want me to tease her and embarrass the shit out of her every time you make her come, I mean I suppose I can, but then which one of us is really looking out for Jill? We'll see you at ten thirty," she said as she waggled her fingers at me in a bitchy wave.

"And don't bring Camila."

"Fine. And if Jill does pick you, I'll let you explain to the rest of the girls how you're Bridgette, and you and Jill have been dating for half the semester. Byeee." She vanished with her middle finger in the air.

I took a deep breath and tried to let my anger out with the air in my lungs. Ginger had some balls acting like I was making an unreasonable request, like feeders being released to new vampires was unheard of. She'd be releasing Jill in a little over a year anyway. The day she graduated she'd be off, probably back to Montreal or to whatever med school was lucky enough to have her, and if things went well, she'd be bound to me. What did it matter if she did it a few months early?

And who cared what the girls in the house thought? I was getting tired of the voice of the group opinions around here. If the other girls didn't like it, tough shit. If my feeders had a problem, oh well, they'd have to get over it. Not everything needed to be a debate. Not everything needed to be open for discussion.

Cleo was bound to the love of her life, and Ginger and Omi and Natasha had come to their true loves the same way. What made their situations any different from mine? Me. That's what. I, Tokyo, the misfit, the outcast, the pain in the ass. I wasn't worthy of my own true love, not until they said. Or so Ginger thought. Jill and I belonged together, and I was going to prove it to her that night.

❖

Jill

Sometimes I wished I had the ability to vanish through walls. I finished my homework at the library before curfew, but I still brought my books to the pantry with me, down the elevator, and through the maze of hallways to Tokyo's apartment, just in case I ran into one of the girls. I'd tell them I was interviewing Tokyo tonight about bondage and sadism since her taste for the two were common enough knowledge around the house, and as far as the girls were concerned, I knew nothing about anything, least of all sex. The type of sex Tokyo liked to have.

All afternoon I had been thinking of this particular sex act I wanted to try. I'd stumbled across it during my legitimate research, but I think it deserved further analysis. I'd been thinking I could ask her flat out, blunt and vulgar the way she liked. Or maybe I could just hint at it, make her draw the information out of me slowly, the other way she liked.

I knocked on her door, just in case she had some unexpected visitor. When I slipped inside, I wasn't wrong. Ginger and Tokyo were sitting on opposite sides of Tokyo's seating area. The air felt like they'd been fighting, there was so much tension between the two of them. Exactly what I didn't want.

"Hi."

"Come sit down a sec," Ginger said, nodding to the pillows strategically placed exactly between them.

"What if I don't want to sit down?"

"You don't have to," she went on, "but we wanted to talk to you about something important so maybe you want to make yourself comfortable."

"I'll stand. Please get to the point. I'm not afraid of you two so you don't have to ease me into whatever this is. Just say it."

"Tokyo would like you to feed her. As in, I release you, you are bound to Tokyo, and she feeds from you. I don't think this is a good idea, but the decision is up to you."

Tokyo didn't let me respond before she jumped in and presented her rebuttal. "You and I are already connected; I just want to make the connection more complete. I want us to really be together."

"No," I said plainly. Tokyo wasn't expecting that.

"What?"

"My answer is no."

And then Ginger jumped back in. "See? What did I tell you? You think you know everything, but she decided and the answer is still no."

"Was the decision ever not going to be mine?"

"No—no. That's not what I meant," Ginger said, trying to back step and failing. "I just told her—"

"Can you leave?"

Ginger's eyebrows shot up. "Me?"

"Yes, you. This actually doesn't have anything to do with you. I'd like to talk to Tokyo alone."

"Nice to see your attitude has rubbed off on her."

"For goodness sake, Ginger! I have my own brain! You're being a jerk, and you're butting into our relationship and I would like to talk to Tokyo alone. You're being rude by insisting you should stay!"

"Wow. Fine. See you two later." Ginger vanished, but her sour attitude was still with us.

I tried to breathe, sinking down against the door. When I looked up, Tokyo was still sitting in the same spot, looking at me like she was waiting for my whole body to detonate. I took another breath.

"You know…you know how I feel about you. But I don't want this."

"Why not?" She wasn't pushing. She just wanted to know; she wanted to understand.

"I've been…struggling with this whole being bound to Ginger thing. I want to help her. I know she needs my blood. I know she needs someone who wants to give her their blood, and I do. But I hate being bound to her. I hate the way it makes me feel about her when it's the exact opposite of exactly how I'm feeling. And I don't want that with you."

"But you said—"

"I do love you, but what if we get into a fight? I don't want to forgive you immediately just because my blood tells me to. I don't want that for you either."

"I think I'm already there. I can't—it's like I can't control it."

"So how much worse does it get for you if we break up and I start seeing someone else? Or you realize that you don't want to be stuck with a vulnerable human? You might get tired of worrying about me all the time. I'm sure it was a huge relief for Camila when Ginger was made fully immortal. I'm always going to be human. Always. And then I'll—" Tokyo knew I'd die one day. There was no point in reminding her.

"What do we do, 'cause I—I want you with me. I don't want you with Ginger anymore."

"And I don't want to be with either of you. Not in that way. I don't want to be in love with my keeper." I banged my head against the door. What had I done? "I have to go."

"We're not—are we—"

"I don't know. I have to go think." The tears were already running down my face. I couldn't handle the tracks of blue suddenly staining Tokyo's cheeks. I scrambled to my feet. I wanted to kiss her so badly, say something that would make us both feel better, but I couldn't.

The walk to the elevator was taking so long that it seemed easier to run. And when I was free of the elevator, it made sense to run to my room, past the girls hanging out on the first floor, and the conversation taking place on the stairs, and the make out session in the hall. I didn't care that Portia was in our room. I didn't care that she was on the phone. I didn't care that she could see me crying. I had nowhere else to go.

"Oh, Jesus. Hold on," I heard her say as I collapsed on my bed. Portia practically spun out of the room she took off so fast.

I wasn't alone for long though. Ginger came to save the day or rub my face in it. I could never tell with her anymore. I let her hug me, and that was sort of okay, though not what I wanted. But then she started talking.

"I'm so sorry, Jill. I tried to tell her."

"Please don't say that. Don't act like you actually care."

"What do you mean? Of course I care." And this was the part I hated. Ginger was the last person I wanted to see right now, but the bond. It took a lot of strength, but I managed to pull away from her and moved to the other end of my bed, wrapping my arms around my knees, trying to keep my insides in my chest. I hated how she had the nerve to be shocked.

"You don't care how I feel, and I hate this because I hate you right now, but we're blood bound so all I want you to do is hold me."

"What do you want me to do? How do I make this better?"

"I don't know!" The sobs came harder now. Why wouldn't she just leave?

You have to make her leave, a tiny voice inside my head said, reminding me of maybe the only upshot of the binding ritual. Vampires loved to be welcomed and they hated it when you took that invite away.

"I remember when I was a freshman and the girls used to make fun of my accent like all the time and tease me about being Canadian, you never stuck up for me."

"Yes. I did."

"No, you didn't really. You would laugh along with them, *while* telling them to stop. But you were laughing at me too. I was there the first time Samantha called me Jaws and you laughed. Tokyo is the only person in this house who doesn't laugh at me, and it's like you're happy that things are screwed up for us right now. You didn't come up here to make me feel better. You came up here to say I told you so. Well, you were right. I got hurt and we might as well be over because I can't give her what she wants. I hope you're happy."

"Jill, I've always wanted what was best for you. I've always looked out for you. I just wanted you to see—"

"That I had no future with Tokyo. I get it. Gosh." I couldn't stop sniffling, even through my cynical laughter. "Being in charge doesn't make you a good person, even if you're right."

She was quiet for a long time, looking at her hands, looking at that giant emerald ring she wore, a clear sign that her love life was a-okay. "I'm sorry," she finally said.

"Please just leave me alone for one minute."

Ginger hesitated a moment and then she vanished. I cried for a while, a long while. I thought the whole fit would subside after some time, but when my whole pathetic, miserable time in the ABO house kept playing over and over in my head, I just couldn't stop.

I was sure the other girls could hear me, maybe even the boys across the street, but I didn't care. About the time I realized

I was actually having a panic attack Camila came and took me in her arms. She was so different when she wasn't around Ginger. Tokyo was right. With Ginger, she was all sex and passion, but alone there was this calmness, this gentle air about her. It soothed me.

"I know," she told me, whispered just so I could hear. "I love her, but I know how she can be. I know she's capable of being wrong. It's okay."

I knew it was, but I was still angry and I still needed space.

"She's young too, you know. And even the rest of us?" Camila said. "We're still learning. We're still human. All the time."

Hearing that helped. Knowing I wasn't the only one who felt this way, knowing that even someone who loved Ginger unconditionally and eternally could still see that she was capable of being really crappy to other human beings.

Camila held me for a long time, rocking me, almost like Papa used to when I was smaller. She stayed with me until I cried myself out and my erratic breathing slowed enough for me to sleep. When I woke a few hours later, she was still there, watching the moon pass over our house, but the next time I opened my eyes, she was gone. Once again, there I was, a new day waiting for me. A day I'd have to face on my own.

❖

Tokyo

I didn't wait for Ginger's round two, or Camila's round one, or Faeth's inspirational lecture on how we should all get along. I went to Hattie's and stayed there for three days. Just as long as I could stay, as long as I could go before I needed more blood.

Chapter Eighteen

Jill

If you were to ask me I would tell you without a doubt that it was much better for your whole sorority to avoid you because they think you're annoying than it was having your whole sorority avoid you because they think you got dumped by some girl in your Arabic class, and instead of taking that semblance of sanity, you have a full nervous breakdown that involves you crying every moment that you aren't actively sitting through a class. I told James and Van that Bridgette and I were fighting. They did their best to make me feel better, but it wasn't working.

I had no idea if Tokyo and I were broken up though. The word around the house was that she'd gone looking for more clues about the body snatching demons that were hunting us down. But I think she was avoiding me. Not that I was reaching out. I wanted to text her, but I had no idea what to say. I couldn't take back the way I turned her down and she couldn't take back the confession of her true feelings.

Tokyo was a vampire. Undead. Bloodthirsty and just as possessive as every other vampire I'd encountered. I loved being with her, but at the end of the day, I didn't want a relationship defined by the blood bond. I wanted Tokyo.

On my way to organic chem lab, I gave in and tried to send her a text. It was a good way to distract myself from the fact that my walking buddies at the moment, Ava and Kait, were ignoring me.

Can we please talk when you come back?

I'm back. We can talk whenever you want.

Not the response I was expecting. I wanted to keep the dialogue between us going, right then and there, but I was approximately a hundred yards from having to clear my head and put on a straight face so I could pay attention for the next ninety minutes.

When I got to lab, I saw a bunch of kids turning around and walking back out. Our TA had cancelled lab. *We'll pick up after the holiday*, the note on the door said.

Why he didn't just e-mail the class was beyond me. My lab was in the Williamsburg building in this odd corner of campus. Having no one to walk with, I headed back to the center of campus. It was cool out, but the sun was shining just enough to sit outside. I figured the center of campus was a safe bet. Ironically, Cleo's memorial bench was wide open.

I sat down and fought the urge to start crying again. Tokyo was back and she hadn't said a word to me. I wondered if she hated me now too. I wondered if she'd really want to speak to me again, or if she just wanted to end things face-to-face. My phone vibrated, but I was instantly crushed. It was a text from Brayley.

I need to stop living like a hoarder. I know the surveys are in my room but I can't find them.

I quickly called her. "Do you want me to come help you look?"

"Yes! Please! I'm sure there's buried treasure in here too. You're welcome to all the booty you can find. I'm in Hamilton Hall, room 913."

I texted James. *Where are you?* I was upset and despondent, but I wasn't stupid.

English, but Tim has a free period I'll have him meet you. Like he promised, a few minutes later, Tim and our other frat brother, Jackson, came and met me on the quad. They were nice enough, asking me how I was doing, but they soon figured out that I wasn't much for conversation. We walked over to Hamilton. "We'll wait down here," Tim said when Brayley let us into the lobby. Hamilton had single-sex floors. so the RAs would freak out if they saw two boys hanging out in the hallway. I hopped in the elevator with Brayley. All I wanted to do was sleep. And talk to Tokyo.

I wanted Tokyo.

Brayley looked as disheveled as her room. Torn sweat pants, no makeup to the point that I saw just how much she usually wore. Half her angled bob was piled on top of her head in a messy bun, and her shirt was dirty. And that was just Brayley.

Her room was a pigsty. It smelled like laundry detergent and her floral perfume, but there was crap everywhere. Clothes, maybe clean, maybe dirty, all over the tile floor. Books, some food wrappers, papers. I saw a hint of a pink and white area rug that ran from under her bed and maybe came out somewhere in the general region of her desk. She had a DSLR camera on a tripod over by her closet. Who knew where the lens cap for that thing was.

"I swear, I had them in my notebook," she whined. I didn't feel bad though. This was literally her own mess and she'd have to fix it, especially if it affected our final presentation.

"Which notebook?" I gave the room another quick scan and spotted at least three spiral bound notebooks. All the same size, all blue.

"The blue one. I scratched HUMAN SEX on the front."

"Okay, great." I dropped my bag next to the door and started rummaging. How could you live this way? "When was the last time you cleaned up?" I asked for my own safety, terrified I'd be the one to stumble across the pizza turned Petri dish that was probably lurking under her bed. "I know this is your room, but it's also a fire hazard."

I overturned a ton of crud on her desk and still nothing. "Bray—" I stood up to find her just staring at me. Not exactly me. More like right above my head. "Brayley."

Nothing, just vacant, blinking eyes. That started losing their color, all of their color until they were completely gray. Her lips started moving, but nothing was coming out.

The protection spell.

I was trying to think of it, the words Tokyo had taught me and made me repeat over and over. It was on the tip of my tongue, right there, but my brain wouldn't spit it out. I'd have the first word and just when the second was coming, the first would vanish. It was the song or the algebraic formula I knew by heart, but when the question was asked, I couldn't come up with the answer. "Frère Jacques." That's what kept coming up. "Frère Jacques." because that was the tune I'd hummed in my head when I was trying to learn the words that could save my life.

Brayley moved, put herself between me and the door. I looked for something, anything I could use to bash her head in. I dove for the tripod, but something slick, a T-shirt or a piece of paper on her tile floor, wiped my foot out from under me. I stumbled to the closet door, knocking over the tripod with my shoulder. My hip and my wrist sang out with pain, but I scrambled for the tripod. That's when I felt Brayley's hands in my hair. I tried to scream as she wrenched me backward, but it came out more like a gasp. She wrenched me closer, getting a good chunk of my hair with the next yank. And then she slammed my head into the floor.

❖

Tokyo

I'd been in the process of packing. Nothing to take, just things to donate. A pile for charity, some stuff I was sure the girls would fight over. At the end of the semester, I was going to move out of the house. I wasn't going to give the girls the truth, just the same story they'd grown accustomed to, Dalhem needed me. I had to hunt down this demon threat. But I'd come back for feedings and our Friday night fun, and then at the end of the year my responsibilities outside of the house would take priority. I'd see Chelsea and Yazmeen off on graduation night and then release the rest of my feeders to Kina and Faeth. I had to get the fuck out of this house and sever my blood ties with the Alpha nest.

I tried to think of reasons to stay, reasons to rise above and put our petty bullshit aside for the sake of the girls, for the greater good. But the more I thought about everything that had gone down between me and Jill, how things had changed between Camila and the horrible shit Ginger had said to me about how my other sister-queens had to just sit by and tell us over and over to play nice, fuck it, it just wasn't worth it. What part of my eternity was meant to be spent this way? What part of my forever was meant to be spent in the company of someone who made me feel like complete shit?

The idea of spending another semester and then another whole year with Jill right under my nose was fucking impossible. I'm sure she would move on, or at least find a way to cope. That was her thing. She got by, but I wouldn't. I still didn't know how it was possible, but she was in my blood now. I could feel her. I felt every moment of every crying jag she'd had over the last few days, felt the way her heart ripped in two the night of our breakup.

How could I live under the same roof and not beg her to let me hold her? Beg her to let me back in. I was crazy for sure; there was no doubt about that. The human in me knew how irrational I was being, but the monster? The demon had already staked its claim, and it wasn't letting go until it was appeased. So yeah, it would be better for everyone if I just left. I hadn't told Ginger or Camila yet, but I was fairly certain they'd be on board with my exit strategy. We were all pretty sick of each other.

I put a pair of rather risky crotchless shorts back in my drawer, thinking maybe I shouldn't donate those, when I felt a noticeable tug. It was deep in my chest, and then I felt something pounding deep in my skull. A struggle. I'd felt it once before, a long time ago.

I vanished to Ginger's apartment. She was there, doubled over, just barely holding on to the couch like she was being hit with labor pains, but instead of holding her stomach, she was gripping her chest. Camila was trying to hold her up.

"It's Jill," she said with a wince.

"I know. Where—"

Just then, Rodrick appeared, eyes wild and glowing, his cell phone pressed to his ear. "Here." He held out the phone and pressed the speaker button. "Our sister-queens are here. Say that again, Timothy."

Tim's shaky voice came through the phone. "Jill! Jill just came out of Hamilton covered in blood! We—we walked her over here to get something from her partner and then she came out, and I think—I think she killed that Brayley chick."

"Oh my God," I said, the breath rushing out of my lungs.

"Where is she now?" Camila said.

"I don't know, like a hundred feet in front of us. It looks like she's heading back toward the house. We don't—something's wrong with her. What should we do?"

"Tell them to stop following her," I said.

"Did you hear that, Timothy? Stay where you are. Don't follow her."

"That demon has her, Tim! I don't want you guys to get hurt!" I yelled so he could hear me.

"Okay, okay. Fuck, there was a lot of blood."

"Go back to Hamilton and wait for the cops or security. I'm sure the lobby monitor called someone already."

"Yeah. Yeah. She did. Fuck. Fuck. Yeah, she was screaming, and I saw her grab the emergency phone as soon as we saw Jill. We'll go back."

Rodrick took them off speaker but refused to hang up. Probably the best idea, just in case whatever had Jill doubled back.

"Come on." I followed as Camila led Ginger into their office. Rodrick was right behind me. Camila helped Ginger into the chair then fired up her security monitors. There was one in every room of the upper floors of the house. They had privacy blind spots, but they did the trick.

At least eleven girls were in the house, D'Monique included. Three girls were with Florencia, watching her stories.

Faeth and Kina appeared and then Omi, right on cue. Camila started giving out orders.

"Faeth, text all the girls and tell them to stay away from the house," she said as she whipped out her own phone. I saw Florencia answer hers a moment later on the monitor. "Get all of the girls out of the house right now. This is a code white. Now!"

Florencia stood calmly but faster than I'd ever seen her move before she was running up the stairs. Girls all over were checking Faeth's text and gathering themselves to get out of the house. Once she had all eleven girls gathered in the foyer, we could see them spilling out the front door and across the street, for the panic room in the OBA house. The front door of the OBA house was open, and Josh was waving the girls in. I felt better for a moment when they were inside, but only for a moment. I could feel Jill and whatever the fuck had her getting closer and closer to the house.

Omi and Kina vanished, and I saw them a second later stepping into the elevator where they changed form and shifted into massive dogs. The emerged in the pantry, ready, waiting when Florencia came running back in the front door. She had a baseball bat in her hand. She closed the door and waited.

❖

It took an eternity. But it was only ten or so minutes before Jill, or a shell of Jill, barged through the door. But it felt like years, and in that time, Cleo arrived.

"Dalhem sent me," was all she said.

Florencia kicked the door closed behind Jill and blocked it, just as Jill swung around, seeing she wasn't alone. Omi and Kina in their canine form slowly crept toward her and, carefully, the three of them started herding Jill toward the pantry. She almost seemed to be cooperating like that was her plan the whole time. But then she turned and tried to lunge at Florencia. Florencia was quick though. She jumped out of the way and swung for Jill.

"Oh, God. Oh please, oh please. Don't hurt her," I said under my breath. The second time, she didn't miss. Florencia clocked Jill in the side of the head and dropped her like a sack of dirty laundry. Omi and Kina went for the hems of her jeans and started pulling Jill toward the pantry. Florencia followed, gripping the bat. Once she was in the elevator and the door closed, I could see Florencia nodding, like she was counting. Of course she knew exactly how long it took the elevator to get to the lower floor. She ran to the emergency panel and hit the button that locked the basement door. Nothing was getting back up to the surface levels. Not unless it could vanish through walls.

❖

The six of us stood in a semicircle facing Jill who was now tied to Camila's office chair. Luckily, I had some extra rope lying around. Her head was bleeding, but not too badly, and her eyes were gray. She was bruised to fuck on the side of her face and her arms. I was sure her back was all scraped up from being dragged. We'd heal her, as soon as we helped her. As soon as this was over.

Ginger still couldn't stand. She was on the couch though, trying to breathe. I felt what she felt, a fist trying to grab my lungs, but somehow for me it was bearable. Ginger, though, she was bound by the blood.

We tried the protection spell. It didn't work. So all that was left was a full-scale exorcism, and only one of us had any firsthand experience with that type of thing.

I turned to Kina. "Okay. So Tarel said they used a rabbit to draw the thing out of Jessi."

"You have to—uh—you have to destroy the vessel." Kina looked like she was going to hurl too.

"Then let's get a rabbit," I said.

"From where?" she asked. "It's fucking high noon, and I know Florencia thinks she's a thug with that bat, but I'm not telling her to set foot back in this house until we're done with this. Not until this thing is gone."

"We have dogs back at the house," Cleo said. Her eyes were eerily focused on Jill. "Dalhem loves those dogs. So does Benny, but they're dogs. And I mean, it's Jill."

I looked at Kina. She was mulling something over. "Whichever one is Dalhem's least favorite—"

"Easy. Kepper."

"Have Leanne's driver bring Kepper down here now and offer our sincerest apologies to the family, but I think they'll understand." She frantically gestured to Jill, who suddenly started laughing. A creepy, thundering laugh, and then she started to speak. Or it. It started to speak. I couldn't understand a thing it was saying.

"What the fuck is that?"

"It's—" Kina took a step closer. Natasha grabbed her arm, but Kina waved her off. "It's the Unspoken." The language of the Angels. None of us knew the tongue of Dalhem and his kindborne. We weren't allowed to know it. It would singe our ears, melt our brains from the inside out, I was told. It was forbidden. But Kina knew.

"What's it saying?" Ginger groaned.

"This is—this isn't the demon that took Jessi. This is something else and he's not going without—"

The demon ground out a final word, like particles of the driest gravel rolling off Jill's tongue.

"Proof. No. A prize."

"It wants to take Jill with it?" Ginger asked. She was crying now. The pain was too much for us both. Jill was in there. I could feel her. She was fighting, but I couldn't tell for how much longer.

"Ginger, you have to release her," I said.

"No! Are you crazy? No!"

"No. Tokyo's right. What do all of these feeders have in common? Us. These things aren't even going after regular bound humans. They are going after humans that are bound to a nest. It's our connection. Maybe if you release her it will be easier to exorcise this thing."

"And what if it kills her?"

"What if we don't try it and it kills her anyway?" Kina said.

"Red. Please." The fear in Camila's voice drew my attention from the gray of Jill's eyes. Camila was terrified—terrified for Jill, but more terrified for Ginger. "Red, let her go. Just for now. You'll get her back, but please try. Let Kina save her."

"Okay. Okay." Ginger looked Jill in the eye for a long, hard moment, probably searching for some shred of evidence that this was the right thing to do. Then she got up from the couch and made her way across the room.

"Don't touch her," Kina said. Ginger didn't respond, but she kept her hands to herself when she bent over to whisper in Jill's ear.

"Jill Marie Babineux, I release you. I release you from the bond you have made to me, my sister-queens, and your sisters. I release you."

Jill and Ginger gasped at the same time, and just as Ginger stood up and reclaimed her strength, Jill's eyes cleared. And then she started screaming.

"Please! Please, let me go! Guys! It's going to kill me! Please—" A deep growl rolled up from her chest, filling her eyes with grayness. I almost threw up. I could still feel Jill, almost stronger than before. She was still in there, still fighting.

"Forget Kepper!" I said. "Get Motherfucker from across the street. I will personally buy the OBA boys another dog. We have to get this thing out of her."

The creature answered me, answering in its forbidden tongue as it focused in my direction. I locked eyes with it.

"Kina."

"It's taking one of us. One of us or the girl. Righteousness is coming to the Earth and—"

"And what?"

"This is only the start. One by one."

CHAPTER NINETEEN

Tokyo

More time passed. Five minutes, an hour. I don't know. Too long for Jill to be sitting there waiting for us to decide what to do, and then I realized way too fucking long for one of us to step up and save her. I looked at my sister-queens and Cleo. Married, married, married to each other, too young and too scared to even move, the only one who knew what the fuck this demon was saying and how to get rid of it, and smarties with a nine-month-old baby. People would miss them, but not many would miss me. Not in any real way.

I stood and paced over to the office door, rolling my neck. An attempt to reach Dalhem across our mental link failed. There was nothing but silence. A silence that let me know there really was no point in waiting. I had to do this now.

"Okay," I said. "Let's do this. Use me."

A combination of "What?", "No!" and, "What the fuck? No!" erupted around the room.

"No," Cleo said with a bit of finality. It didn't matter though. My mind was made up.

"For once, we're not gonna make a decision as a group. And, Cleo, you don't even live here anymore so your vote doesn't count."

"If I'm Dalhem's proxy then my vote counts." That explained a lot. Our Master was purposefully off our grid.

"And if Dalhem knew I wanted to sacrifice myself for one of the girls, he would hate it, but he would say yes. Ginger, give Hattie clearance to the house. We're running out of time and I want to say good-bye."

"I don't like this," Kina said.

"I know, but we can't do this to Jill, just sit here and wait and debate. I felt Rory's terror after she'd been half-possessed by this thing for one minute. So how long do we wait before this does irreversible damage to Jill's mind, to her soul? You want to draw straws?"

"It should be me," Ginger said. Camila's whole body tensed up beside her, and I almost laughed. Like Camila would let her go.

"No. You're always saying I need to step up and take responsibility, show how much I care for the girls—"

"This is not what I meant! You don't have anything to prove."

Hattie appeared, just as shocked and confused as the rest of my sisters. I crossed the room and took her hand. "You still don't get it. I love her. I want to do this *for* her. Saving the rest of you from uncertain death is just a bonus." Finally, I turned and faced Hattie. Tears were already lining her eyes. She wasn't dumb. She knew what this was.

"Thank you. Thank you for giving me this amazing second life. Thank you for loving me," I told her.

She leaned forward just enough, her forehead touching mine. "And I'm so proud of what you've done with that life. Your blood-ties sustained me. Save this young woman. The universe will embrace you for it."

I broke down and pulled her into my arms. "Please take care of Ansley and Juniper. Tell them I love them and I'm sorry."

"I will. I swear it."

I held on for another long minute. No one had loved me the way Hattie had, not even Dalhem, 'cause her love for me went beyond the blood we shared. Hattie was my true friend.

"Okay." I stepped away from my maker, wiping my face ten or twenty times. "We've got to kill me proper, right? Head and heart?"

"Uh, either should do it," Kina said. "Both might be overkill."

"Let's do the heart. I'll only be whole for like three seconds after you get it out, but I like my head where it is. We need a human, right? And what time is sunset?"

"Four thirty," Faeth said. "Twenty minutes."

"Well, fuck. Get Florencia on standby and let's do this."

There was hesitation all around the room. That shit was not gonna work. "Listen, if we don't do this now you run the risk of having a possessed vampire on your hands all night. Or we leave Jill like this till sunup. You all decide, but we are on a tight schedule here."

Camila vanished and was back a moment later with one of her ceremonial daggers, used for superficial flesh wounds. Hopefully, it could cut through a rib cage.

"Tokyo, once the jump is complete, you have to fight, okay?" Kina said. "Don't relax. Don't surrender. Don't let it take you. It won't take long to get your heart out, but if this thing takes over, we won't just have a possessed vampire on our hands. We'll have a possessed vampire who knows how to use your powers, who knows all your strengths and weaknesses, where all your feeders live, with the ability to vanish at sunset. Don't let this thing win."

"Okay." I let out another deep breath. "Okay. If I die, that'll automatically release the girls from our blood bond. So yeah, okay. Let's do this."

"Tokyo—" Faeth said.

"Oh, for fuck's sake!" My eyes started leaking uncontrollably. I wasn't crying. I was weeping, 'cause what the fuck. "I love all of you guys. Even you, Ginger. You asshole. I love you and I'll miss you. Just take care of the girls. Tell them I'm sorry. Oh, and Moreland too. I'm holding forty grand for one of her feeders so make sure he gets that."

Ginger laughed through her tears. "Yeah. We'll handle it."

I walked over to Jill, but Omi stopped me and hugged me, then kissed me on the lips. Then Faeth, then Natasha, then Kina and Ginger and Camila. Cleo didn't move from her spot by the couch, but she was in my head. No words, just pure, uncut emotion. Everything that needed to be said flooded the walls of my veins.

"I'll make sure Dalhem knows exactly what you did here," she said for the others to hear. It was all that was left to say.

Kina had me lie down on the floor with my feet touching Jill's. Then she had Omi, Faeth, Natasha, and Ginger all take a limb. I had to fight, and they had to finish the job.

Kina said the words, the spell in the tongue of the Angels that would free us all. My body started to burn as she said the same words over and over. I tasted burning wood and this time, flesh. And then, for the second time in almost two hundred years, I died.

❖

Jill

I woke up tied to a chair with the worst taste in my mouth. The smell of something burning. Tokyo. Our sister-queens were holding her down. She was flailing, fighting, and Camila was stabbing her in the chest. A massive pool of blood was forming on the carpet. Tokyo's blood.

"What are you doing? Let me go! You're killing her!"

"Jill! Hold on. Let me help you." I looked up and Hattie was there. She rushed over to my side and started untying my restraints.

"What's going on? Stop!" I yelled at Camila, but it was too late. Her hand was in Tokyo's chest. Inside her chest. I heard a sickening pop, and when she pulled her arm back, she was holding Tokyo's heart. Tokyo stopped struggling.

"Tokyo saved you. That demon got you."

"So you guys ripped out her heart?" I was finally free from the chair. I rushed to Tokyo's side, but it was already too late. Tokyo was dead. "She took the demon from me?"

"Yes. She wouldn't let it go down any other way," Cleo said, somewhere in the distance. There was a hurricane roaring in my ears.

"Five minutes, you guys. Florencia is waiting outside," Faeth said.

"Waiting for what?" I looked up as Camila was crossing the room with Tokyo's heart. "Wait!"

"Jill, we have to destroy this or else that demon will stick around in Tokyo's body," Ginger explained.

"Destroy it how?"

"In the sun. I'm sorry, Jill, but the sun's setting. We have to get this thing out of here," Camila said. She opened the door. Florencia was waiting, ready to take the heart. The part of Tokyo that mattered to me the most.

"No!"

I stood, letting go of Tokyo's clammy hand.

"Jill. We don't have time."

"Let me do it."

Camila paused, probably checking in with Ginger or debating whether or not she should hand me the beating heart of my now dead girlfriend.

"Okay. Come on."

I followed Camila down the hall. We ran all the way to the underground garage. I had no clue there was an emergency storm door, but Camila showed me the secret exit. And then she handed me the heart. "The code is 3681. Then straight into the sun. Don't hesitate."

"Okay. Okay. Oh, my goodness."

Camila shoved me through the inner door. I was in the dark for just a second until an emergency light came on revealing a short set of stairs. At the top was a door with a keypad. My bloody fingers managed the code. I made it outside and found only a small patch of sunlight left near the rear fence. I could hear sirens, police sirens and helicopters overhead, nearby, but I ignored them and ran for the fence, thinking if I hurried I'd have some time to say good-bye. A moment to at least tell this last bit of the best thing that had ever happened to me that I loved her and I always would. But the moment I stepped into that sliver of sunlight, Tokyo's heart ignited in my hands and instantly turned to ash.

❖

The dark and the cold told me it was time to go inside, but I couldn't move. How long had I been out there, letting my tears run into a pile of ashes? I hadn't the faintest idea. Eventually, Faeth came and carried me back inside. I didn't fight her. I was cold and covered in ash and blood. We didn't go back to Ginger and Camila's; the cleanup was probably underway.

She took me to her place, with her clean modern furniture and colors and whites. No black to be seen. I washed and dressed in a gigantic shirt she let me borrow. She wrapped me in a blanket and pulled me into her side on the sofa, letting her tall frame be my shelter. We watched cartoons. Cartoons were safe.

Omi brought me something to eat. Hattie had to take care of some things, she said. But she would be back to check on me. She'd be back soon.

Then Ginger came, to deprogram me I supposed. I'd seen hell in that thing. Seen horrors. I'd killed my presentation partner. If Ginger didn't come in and unscramble my brains, I'd probably never sleep again. She smiled and approached me slowly, held out her hand cautiously, her knife in the other, asking if I'd take her back, if I'd be bound to her once again.

I looked at Ginger and her own stretched hands, then up to her green eyes. I thought about this moment two years earlier, and what I should have said, the questions I should have asked.

She said the words exactly the same way, posed a question that had a clear and definite answer. "Jill, will you bind yourself to me—"

"No."

"Huh?"

"No. I don't want you."

"Jill, please. I know things are…things are fucked right now, but I only released you to save you. We need to reseal our bond."

"For what?"

"So I can—"

"Feed from me? We don't need a bond for that. You want to keep tabs on me, and we've seen how well that worked out. I don't want to be bound to you or anyone else."

Ginger looked at me, mouth open, but silent. If I had to move out of the house, I would. Dorm living wouldn't be so bad. At least I'd have my own room. Moving wasn't happening tonight though. I closed my eyes and leaned my head against Faeth's side. It was strange, but I had no trouble sleeping at all.

❖

A lot of work went into covering up a crime scene, but Dalhem had the resources and the connections. Faeth and Camila had taken responsibility for looking after me and making sure I didn't go off the deep end, and while they were hovering, I made them answer my questions. I wanted to know everything that was going on. I had a right to know. So they told me. I killed Brayley. Well, the demon used my body to kill Brayley, and at least two dozen people saw me make my way back to the Row covered in her blood. The first thing they had to do was find anyone who saw anything; at the same time, Omi was working with local police to cover up her murder.

It had to be done. I understood the necessity of the work, the secrets, the lies. I also didn't want to go to prison. But I had a feeling I would also struggle with the guilt of knowing that Brayley's family would never know what really happened.

Not that they would understand. I imagine losing a child was hard enough to comprehend, but how would they handle the grisly details, details that wouldn't make sense. Camila explained that homicide investigations took time, so for now they believed her murder to be a complete accident. Omi and Mary had been there when Brayley's parents came to identify her body. They altered things, made them see the still, yet peaceful, body of their daughter. Not the mangled corpse I'd left behind in Hamilton. Eventually, they'd find someone, someone who had actually committed a murder and attribute Brayley's death to them to give her family some closure. If closure was really possible.

And while all of this was going on outside the house, my sisters in Alpha Beta Omega did their best to deal with Tokyo's death. I made it clear that I didn't want my personal association with Tokyo to be disclosed to the girls because I knew they would blame me. Not to mention the massive can of worms we'd be opening if the girls realized who Bridgette really was. Camila and Ginger were nice enough to explain that Tokyo chose to sacrifice herself for me. That was the point of all of this, Camila said. So they could protect us, shield us, do whatever it took to keep us safe. There were some grumblings about why Ginger hadn't taken the fall since I was her feeder, at the time, but that kind of talk was quickly shut down when Chelsea admitted that Tokyo was exactly the kind of person to die for one of us, any of us. Chelsea knew just how special she was.

Her feeders in ABO were split between Ginger and Camila. Faeth told me that Hattie had taken her feeders outside of the house. I felt a little better knowing they were being cared for by someone who was just as amazing and caring as the vampire they had lost.

Being possessed seemed reason enough for me to be acting a little out of it. The girls tiptoed around me, not speaking to me directly, but showing this sudden deference to my well-being. Portia asked me what I needed every morning and every night when she saw me. Someone was always there, when Faeth and Camila couldn't be, making sure I ate. I could always feel Florencia watching me. When I cried silently, they didn't push me away, but pulled me closer, encouraging me to be with them. I didn't fight it, didn't have the strength to.

Everything I had in me was focused on not playing the blame game. I didn't kill Tokyo. This wasn't my fault. But I would never see her again. I would never get an opportunity to tell her how sorry I was. We would never have a chance to at least try to work things out. I didn't want to be bound to anyone, but I wanted her in my life, still. I wanted to be with her, and now all hope of seeing just where the love between us could go was gone. I thought about her almost every minute. Saw her heart literally in my hands, over and over. Knew the smell of her hot ashes would never leave me.

Faeth offered to follow me home to Montreal for Thanksgiving break, but I said no. I needed a break from our sister-queens. I needed a break from the undead, from those whose only ties to me involved blood magic. I needed a break from Ginger's not-so-subtle hovering, and she needed to understand that she wasn't going to get me back. I never wanted to be bound to her again. Dad and Papa knew something was wrong the moment they found me in baggage claim. A breakup, I'd told them, backing up the existence of a relationship with the pictures of Bridgette and me I still had in my phone. They understood.

Dr. Miller e-mailed me over break. I'd received an A in her class, she said. She'd understand if she didn't see me for the rest of the semester. I thought about not going back. I could stay home with Papa and Dad, relax, regroup, bake. But something told me I had to go back. Something felt unfinished. Something other than my degrees. Decisions had to be made, decisions about my future with Alpha Beta Omega.

Chapter Twenty

Jill

A break proved to be exactly what I needed. Being home gave me time to think, and my parents being the amazing people they are, gave me the time I needed to mourn, even if they thought my tears were caused by the end of a relationship and not someone I loved more than I had given myself a chance to comprehend. When I came back to campus after that short week away, I had a better sense of what I needed to move forward. I'd planned to talk to Ginger as soon as I put my stuff up.

Portia was in our room, eating takeout on her bed.

"Hey! How was your Thanksgiving?"

"We celebrate it in October in Canada. But it was nice to go home."

"Oh. Well, was there food at least?"

"There is always food."

"You want to try some of this? We stopped at this Jamaican place on our way back." I thought about saying no and getting on with what I needed to do. I still had to prepare for class. As a survivor, I'd gotten a pass from the chancellor's office. I could have stayed home for the rest of the semester, but I had already studied too hard to skip finals. I was earning my 4.0. But I was hungry, and Portia had been pretty nice to me.

I sat on her bed and took a forkful of oxtails and rice. "Oh. That is good."

"Hey, Jill." I looked up as Ava knocked on our doorframe. "Bridgette's downstairs."

"Back for more," Portia commented absently, but I couldn't speak or move.

"You heard me, right? Your girlfriend is downstairs."

"I thought you guys broke up," Portia said.

"Oh yeah, didn't you?" Ava said.

"I—uh—yeah. We broke up. Are you sure it's her?"

"I mean I've seen her before and I've talked to her before, and just now, the darnedest thing, she comes to the door and says is Jill around? Can you tell her Bridgette's here?"

"You want me to get her to kick rocks?" Portia asked with a little too much excitement in her eyes. She probably thought she owed Bridgette for all the nights I'd cried her out of the room. That would have been fine and good if it made the slightest bit of sense. One, Tokyo was dead. Two, it was two in the afternoon and the sun was very much out and shining, even if it was really chilly. There was also the small issue of Tokyo being dead. Her heart had turned to ash and her whole body crumbled to the same black and gray dust moments later. Dead. As in absolutely dead.

"You gonna go down or...?"

"Yeah. No. Yes, I'll be right down. Thanks."

"You need backup?" Portia asked as I was putting my shoes back on. "Because I'll let her know."

"No, I got this." Whatever was going on did not need spectators.

Walking down the stairs seemed impossible. I wanted to run, close this distance between us as fast as I could, but all I could anticipate was disappointment. What if it was a trick or a ghost or a super cruel prank? What if grief had driven me crazy and this was all happening in my mind? There was no one waiting for me. Just...

Bridgette was standing in the foyer talking to Aleeka. Skinny jeans, high-top sneakers, and a Maryland University hoodie. Her hair was up in a messy bun, and she looked exhausted, like she hadn't slept in days. Or like she'd been dead. I walked up to them. I stopped just close enough, close enough to kiss her face.

"And she's here. Talk to you later," Aleeka said before she bounced away. She had no clue.

"Hi," she said. Same voice. Same face. Same height as me. Same sweet sincerity, but something was different about that sweetness. This time she would absolutely care which way I reacted. There was one thing she needed to hear from me. But she had some talking to do first.

She watched me carefully, watched my hand as I reached between us and touched her fingers. They were cold, but normal cold like she'd just come from outside. Human cold.

I didn't cry, but a few tears leaked out of my left eye, then my right.

"Can we go outside?" she asked.

"Yes."

She opened the door with familiarity, not like she was a visitor, and held it open for me.

It was colder than I remembered, but the sun was still shining. The porch was in full shade, but she stepped out after me, closing the door, and then went for the stairs that were bathing her in bright rays of light. And nothing happened. I could see the different shades of brown in her hair.

I sat down, then turned to face her. I needed to keep looking at her to know she was real. She looked up and wiped my face with her fingertips.

"I died. I definitely died. All of that happened. I can't tell you what happened after. What I saw, what I heard. I tried to tell Hattie, and my tongue physically can't do it."

"Hattie knows you're okay?"

"Yeah, she came last night."

"Where? Where did you see her?"

"Moreland's. I still have my places, and my bank accounts are more like trust funds now, but I feel comfortable at Moreland's."

My whole body was shaking, and my face was hot. I felt pressure in my stomach, my throat, behind my eyes. Sensation overload. Too much information all at once that didn't make sense. "What's going on?"

"The best I can understand it, I got one last chance."

"At what exactly?" I asked.

"Life? I'm not a vampire anymore, as you can see. No more fangs. No blood cravings." She turned her hand palm up. "I can handle the sun just fine." She made a fist. "But I can still do this." The skin on her hand was suddenly covered in bright blue feathers. When she shook her arm, her hand went back to normal.

"So did you take this form to trick the girls, so you could get close to me?"

"This is my natural form. The real Miyoko. Body and soul forever mine to keep. I'm cute, huh?"

"Yes, you are."

"I can vanish too, but—"

"But what?"

"I like walking during the day."

"Hmm. So you're a witch."

She laughed. The same laugh. I leaned forward and covered my face, and then she did exactly what I wanted her to do, she put her arm around my back. She kissed the side of my head.

"I'm mortal. Mortal with powers, but mortal. Mortal plus."

I laughed this time. "I like the way that sounds." I looked up. Her eyes were so clear, bright brown in the sun.

"I'm just a regular Japanese-American girl. Orphaned, but with friends all over the world. I'm dying, like normal people do, slowly, day by day, walking toward my true end. But I can feel you still."

"You can?"

"Yeah. Right in my heart, still in my blood. I think that's why they sent me back. For you, to be with you. I think this is my heaven."

"Oh, my goodness!" I covered my face again.

"Too much? Do I need to ask a girl out on a regular date first before I tell a twenty-year-old I want to spend the rest of my life with her? That I'd die for her over and over again? More flowers and a six-pack of grape soda? We can start there."

"No, no. This is good. What will you do?"

"Not sure yet. I don't have to do anything, but I should. I told Moreland I want to."

"You're bound to her?"

"Yeah. I need—I need to stay connected. It feels safer. You? You feel—unattached."

"I am. I'm not sure if I want to go back, but I know what I know. I don't want three years of my life gone if I say bye for good, and I don't want to move out."

"Moreland always has room at her place, or just…with her."

"It's not a bad idea. I like her. I'd pick her if I had the choice."

"You do."

"And us?"

"That's your choice too, baby."

"I choose you." And then we were kissing. Softly. Slowly. Being gentle with each other for all the right reasons. Her cheeks were cold when I touched them, but now so were mine.

"Have you told Ginger yet?"

"No, but I will. With my powers, she'll have to give me access to the house if I want to poof in and out to see you. Especially in the middle of the night. Say, if I have to help you with any more presentations."

"You want to go talk to her now?" I wanted to get the conversation over with, and I wanted Miyoko in my bed. She exhaled and slid her hand between my legs.

"Soon. I just want to sit out here with you for a couple more minutes."

"We can do that."

"And then I'll make you scream."

"We can do that too. I love you."

"I needed to hear that, baby. I love you too."

THE END

About the Author

Raised in Southern New Hampshire, Rebekah Weatherspoon now lives in Southern California. Before moving west, she received a BA in English literature with a concentration in Shakespearean works from the University of North Carolina at Charlotte.

Rebekah Weatherspoon writes erotic romance, both paranormal and contemporary, New Adult and Adult. Her BDSM romance, *At Her Feet*, won the Golden Crown Literary Award for erotic lesbian fiction and most recently her novella, *FIT (#1 in the FIT Trilogy)*, won the Romantic Times Book Reviews Reviewers' Choice Award for Best Erotica Novella. You can find out more about Rebekah and her books at www.rebekahweatherspoon.com.

Books Available from Bold Strokes Books

24/7 by Yolanda Wallace. When the trip of a lifetime becomes a pitched battle between life and death, will anyone survive? (978-1-62639-6-197)

A Return to Arms by Sheree Greer. When a police shooting makes national headlines, activists Folami and Toya struggle to balance their relationship and political allegiances, a struggle intensified after a fiery young artist enters their lives. (978-1-62639-6-814)

After the Fire by Emily Smith. Paramedic Connor Haus is convinced her time for love has come and gone, but when firefighter Logan Curtis comes into town, she learns it may not be too late after all. (978-1-62639-6-524)

Dian's Ghost by Justine Saracen. The road to genocide is paved with good intentions. (978-1-62639-5-947)

Fortunate Sum by M. Ullrich. Financial advisor Catherine Carter lives a calculated life, but after a collision with spunky Imogene Harris (her latest client) and unsolicited predictions, Catherine finds herself facing an unexpected variable: Love. (978-1-62639-5-305)

Soul to Keep by Rebekah Weatherspoon. What *won't* a vampire do for love... (978-1-62639-6-166)

When I Knew You by KE Payne. Eight letters, three friends, two lovers, one secret. Can the past ever be forgiven? (978-1-62639-5-626)

Wild Shores by Radclyffe. Can two women on opposite sides of an oil spill find a way to save both a wildlife sanctuary and their hearts? (978-1-62639-6-456)

Love on Tap by Karis Walsh. Beer and romance are brewing for Tace Lomond when archaeologist Berit Katsaros comes into her life. (987-1-162639-564-0)

Love on the Red Rocks by Lisa Moreau. An unexpected romance at a lesbian resort forces Malley to face her greatest fears where she must choose between playing it safe or taking a chance at true happiness. (987-1-162639-660-9)

Tracker and the Spy by D. Jackson Leigh. There are lessons for all when Captain Tanisha is assigned untried pyro Kyle and a lovesick dragon horse for a mission to track the leader of a dangerous cult. (987-1-162639-448-3)

Whirlwind Romance by Kris Bryant. Will chasing the girl break Tristan's heart or give her something she's never had before? (987-1-162639-581-7)

Whiskey Sunrise by Missouri Vaun. Culture and religion collide when Lovey Porter, daughter of a local Baptist minister, falls for the handsome thrill-seeking moonshine runner, Royal Duval. (987-1-162639-519-0)

Dyre: By Moon's Light by Rachel E. Bailey. A young werewolf, Des, guards the aging leader of all the Packs: the Dyre. Stable employment—nice work, if you can get it…at least until silver bullets start to fly. (978-1-62639-6-623)

Fragile Wings by Rebecca S. Buck. In Roaring Twenties London, can Evelyn Hopkins find love with Jos Singleton or will the scars of the Great War crush her dreams? (978-1-62639-5-466)

Live and Love Again by Jan Gayle. Jessica Whitney could be Sarah Jarret's second chance at love, but their differences and Sarah's grief continue to come between their budding relationship. (978-1-62639-5-176)

Starstruck by Lesley Davis. Actress Cassidy Hayes and writer Aiden Darrow find out the hard way not all life-threatening drama is confined to the TV screen or the pages of a manuscript. (978-1-62639-5-237)

Stealing Sunshine by Tina Michele. Under the Central Florida sun, two women struggle between fear and love as a dangerous plot of deception and revenge threatens to steal priceless art and lives. (978-1-62639-4-452)

The Fifth Gospel by Michelle Grubb. Hiding a Vatican secret is dangerous—sharing the secret suicidal—can Felicity survive a perilous book tour, and will her PR specialist, Anna, be there when it's all over? (978-1-62639-4-476)

Cold to the Touch by Cari Hunter. A drug addict's murder is the start of a dangerous investigation for Detective Sanne Jensen and Dr. Meg Fielding, as they try to stop a killer with no conscience. (978-1-62639-526-8)

Forsaken by Laydin Michaels. The hunt for a killer teaches one woman that she must overcome her fear in order to love, and another that success is meaningless without happiness. (978-1-62639-481-0)

Infiltration by Jackie D. When a CIA breach is imminent, a Marine instructor must stop the attack while protecting her heart from being disarmed by a recruit. (978-1-62639-521-3)

Midnight at the Orpheus by Alyssa Linn Palmer. Two women desperate to make their way in the world, a man hell-bent on revenge, and a cop risking his career: all in a day's work in Capone's Chicago. (978-1-62639-607-4)

Spirit of the Dance by Mardi Alexander. Major Sorla Reardon's return to her family farm to heal threatens Riley Johnson's safe life when small-town secrets are revealed, and love may not conquer all. (978-1-62639-583-1)

Sweet Hearts by Melissa Brayden, Rachel Spangler, and Karis Walsh. Do you ever wonder *Whatever happened to...*? Find out when you reconnect with your favorite characters from Melissa Brayden's *Heart Block*, Rachel Spangler's *LoveLife*, and Karis Walsh's *Worth the Risk*. (978-1-62639-475-9)

Totally Worth It by Maggie Cummings. Who knew there's an all-lesbian condo community in the NYC suburbs? Join twentysomething BFFs Meg and Lexi at Bay West as they navigate friendships, love, and everything in between. (978-1-62639-512-1)

Illicit Artifacts by Stevie Mikayne. Her foster mother's death cracked open a secret world Jil never wanted to see…and now she has to pick up the stolen pieces. (978-1-62639-472-8)

Pathfinder by Gun Brooke. Heading for their new homeworld, Exodus's chief engineer Adina Vantressa and nurse Briar Lindemay carry game-changing secrets that may well cause them to lose everything when disaster strikes. (978-1-62639-444-5)

Prescription for Love by Radclyffe. Dr. Flannery Rivers finds herself attracted to the new ER chief, city girl Abigail Remy, and the incendiary mix of city and country, fire and ice, tradition and change is combustible. (978-1-62639-570-1)

Ready or Not by Melissa Brayden. Uptight Mallory Spencer finds relinquishing control to bartender Hope Sanders too tall an order in fast-paced New York City. (978-1-62639-443-8)

Summer Passion by MJ Williamz. Women loving women is forbidden in 1946 Hollywood, yet Jean and Maggie strive to keep their love alive and away from prying eyes. (978-1-62639-540-4)

The Princess and the Prix by Nell Stark. "Ugly duckling" Princess Alix of Monaco was resigned to loneliness until she met racecar driver Thalia d'Angelis. (978-1-62639-474-2)

Winter's Harbor by Aurora Rey. Lia Brooks isn't looking for love in Provincetown, but when she discovers chocolate croissants and pastry chef Alex McKinnon, her winter retreat quickly starts heating up. (978-1-62639-498-8)

The Time Before Now by Missouri Vaun. Vivian flees a disastrous affair, embarking on an epic, transformative journey to escape her past, until destiny introduces her to Ida, who helps her rediscover trust, love, and hope. (978-1-62639-446-9)

Twisted Whispers by Sheri Lewis Wohl. Betrayal, lies, and secrets—whispers of a friend lost to darkness. Can a reluctant psychic set things right or will an evil soul destroy those she loves? (978-1-62639-439-1)

The Courage to Try by C.A. Popovich. Finding love is worth getting past the fear of trying. (978-1-62639-528-2)

Break Point by Yolanda Wallace. In a world readying for war, can love find a way? (978-1-62639-568-8)

Countdown by Julie Cannon. Can two strong-willed, powerful women overcome their differences to save the lives of seven others and begin a life they never imagined together? (978-1-62639-471-1)

Keep Hold by Michelle Grubb. Claire knew some things should be left alone and some rules should never be broken, but the most forbidden, well, they are the most tempting. (978-1-62639-502-2)

Deadly Medicine by Jaime Maddox. Dr. Ward Thrasher's life is in turmoil. Her partner Jess left her, and her job puts her in the path of a murderous physician who has Jess in his sights. (978-1-62639-424-7)

New Beginnings by KC Richardson. Can the connection and attraction between Jordan Roberts and Kirsten Murphy be enough for Jordan to trust Kirsten with her heart? (978-1-62639-450-6)